FURY—STALLION OF BROKEN WHEEL RANCH

With hearts pounding and breath quickening, the men lowered the rope to the ground and stared toward the silvered hills. Not four hundred yards away, they saw him coming! Fury—the ebony king of the range!

The most magnificent horse Jim Newton had ever seen! From great tossing head to long, sweeping tail, the stallion stood at least fifteen hands high—every inch of him jet black. King of all he surveyed, Fury was unquestionably the leader of the mustang herd grazing on the new spring grass of the plateau. Jim knew that here was a horse his Broken Wheel Ranch must have.

Catching Fury, however, was not going to be easy. He was much too cagey, just like the "ghost horses" the ranch hands talked about. A trap for Fury had to be baited. The Broken Wheel's reputation was at stake. Jim could not allow this coal-black stallion that breathed fire and fury to be captured for any other ranch.

How the fiery mustang stallion became an important part of the Broken Wheel Ranch is only part of this fast-moving story. The thrilling account of life on a horse ranch and a breath-taking description of the fight for Fury's life also make this a book sure to hold the attention of everyone who loves a good horse story.

This TEMPO BOOKS *edition contains the complete text of the original hard-cover edition.*

FURY
Stallion of Broken Wheel Ranch
by Albert G. Miller

tempo
books

GROSSET & DUNLAP

A National General Company
Publishers   New York

Contents

CHAPTER 1

Ruler of the Wild Herd

JIM NEWTON brought his mount to a sudden stop, turned in the saddle, and lifted a forefinger to his lips. His ranch foreman Pete, who was riding a couple of lengths behind, pulled up short, his mouth silently forming the word "what?"

Jim turned forward again and pointed. Old Pete craned his short neck, but saw nothing out of the ordinary. Frowning, he stood up in his stirrups, so as to reach Jim's eye-level; and his leathery face broke into a wide grin. Beyond a distant rocky ledge, forty or fifty wild horses were grazing on the new spring grass of the plateau. The mustang herd had spent the winter in the high country, and the tender, green growth tasted like a banquet after a long period on short rations.

The men watched in silence for a moment, then uttered soft exclamations of surprise. At the far edge of the cluster of animals, a jetblack stallion had come into view. Slowly and protectively, he was circling the herd of mares. Jim and Pete knew that he was their leader and ruler, and, as they eyed him in quiet excitement, both men thought him the most magnificent horse they had ever seen. From great tossing head to long sweeping tail, the stallion stood at least fifteen hands high, and every square inch of him was the color of anthracite.

Pete's eyes glistened with admiration. "Jee—hosha-phat!" he whispered. "Jee—*jumpin'*—hoshaphat!"

"You said it," Jim muttered. Automatically, his hand reached down and rested on his coiled lariat.

Pete caught the gesture from the corner of his eye. "Not a chance, Jim."

Jim spoke softly but eagerly. "But we can try, mis-ter—we can sure try."

The older man nodded. "Shore," he muttered, "we could try ropin' a tornado, too."

"Before we move we've got to let them know we're here. A sudden motion will scare them, and they'll take off." Jim cupped his left hand around his mouth. "Hey there!" he called. "Hey!"

The stallion made a guttural sound and froze, peer-ing alertly in Jim's direction. The heads of the nervous herd jerked up together.

"Now," Jim said, "move in slowly."

Standing motionless, the anxious herd watched the two riders approaching. When only fifty yards sepa-rated the men from the wild horses, the tension broke as the black leader uttered an angry scream and charged through the center of the herd, which opened swiftly to give him running room. Jim and Pete felt their mounts shudder with fright beneath them. The saddle horses wanted desperately to turn and take off. The challenging stallion plunged toward them like a dark streak, but before he reached them he came to a sudden halt, swung his great head around, and voiced a shrill command. The herd wheeled obediently and raced from the plateau into the safety of the forest.

Pete shook his head in admiration. "He shore knows how to handle 'em."

"And how," Jim chuckled.

The black beast now faced the men squarely, as though daring them to make a move. He was like a belligerent boy inviting another one to cross a line in the dust, at the risk of getting a broken jaw or a black eye. Jim and Pete stared back at him, transfixed with wonder.

"What a horse!" Jim muttered. "This is one animal I've just got to have!"

"By the look on his face," Pete said, "he's gotta have you, too—in his teeth."

The wrathful stallion now sprang into action and began a mad war dance. Swinging his head into the air, he jumped high off the ground a half-dozen times, roaring challenges from his deep chest. Finally, having told his human enemies of his bravery and contempt, he turned and raced off to join the herd.

"Come on, Pete—let's chase him!" Jim cried.

Pete snorted. "*You* chase him. But first git yerself one-a them jet airy-o-planes."

Jim realized that the horse he was riding was no match for the stallion in speed. "I guess you're right. It would be like trying to catch a bolt of lightning with a pogo stick." He pounded his fist into his saddle. "I'm going to have that stallion, Pete, do you hear? I'm not going to rest till I've got him in the corral at the Broken Wheel Ranch."

"I know jest how ya feel, Jim. I'm a purty old coot, an' I've been around horses all my life. But I've never laid eyes on the likes of that one. *Never*."

Jim's powerful jaw was set. "I'm going to capture that baby. You just wait and see."

"I shore hope so. I want the critter jest as bad as you do."

Pete pushed his hat back. "Gosh-a-mighty—did you ever see a horse so full of fire and fury?"

"Fury!" Jim's eyes glistened. "That's *it!*"

"*What's* it?"

"That's his name! You just gave it to him! Fury!"

Pete grinned. "Fury. . . . Hm—not bad, Jim, not bad at all. Fury—of the Broken Wheel Ranch!"

Catching wild horses was Jim Newton's business. His Broken Wheel Ranch was an outfit that roped horses on the range and broke them for saddle or harness. He made his living by selling the animals to ranchers all over the state, even to the owners of the big spreads; wealthy men, such as Charlie Stevens. Stevens owned an elaborate layout at the opposite end of the valley, about ten miles north of the Broken Wheel.

The morning after Jim and Pete had their first encounter with the wild black stallion, Charlie Stevens rode down to the BW Ranch to pick up a string of mares that Jim had broken for him. Pete met Stevens at the gate and told him excitedly about the adventure with the leader of the wild herd. But even though Stevens respected Pete's judgment and knowledge of horseflesh, he was a trifle skeptical until he heard the story again from Jim himself.

Later, the three men stood on the front porch of the ranchhouse, discussing the stallion. Stevens was asking questions.

"You say he stands fifteen hands high?"

Jim nodded. "At least."

"Mebbe sixteen," Pete said enthusiastically. "Me an' Jim didn't git a fair chance to measure him yesterday. The big critter wouldn't hold still long enough." His eyes twinkled. "Besides, we didn't have our tape measure along."

Charlie Stevens squinted across the valley into the hills. "From what you men tell me, he sounds like a horse worth owning."

"There's none better," Jim said. "And I'm going to own him, Charlie." He half closed his eyes, as though he could already see the stallion in the corral. "Someday you'll come riding down here, and Fury will be standing right there inside that fence."

Stevens raised his eyebrows. "Fury? Don't tell me you've already got him branded and named."

"Well, maybe not branded just yet—but he's named. Pete gave me the idea yesterday when the stallion was jumping around, cussing in horse language and roaring fire and fury at us."

"That's a fact," Pete said proudly. "Ya might say I was the sponsor at that stallion's christenin'. Jest wait'll ya see him, Charlie. You'll say, like us, that Fury's the only name in the book fer a bundle of dynamite like him."

The visitor scratched his chin. "Well, if Fury's as wild and mean as you men say, I doubt whether I ever will see him. At least, not here in your corral."

"Don't bet on that," Jim warned.

"But how're you going to get close enough to rope him? According to you fellows he runs like the wind. You're going to have to be riding horses as fast as he is."

"Gosh, I reckon yer right," Pete said, crestfallen. He looked at Jim and frowned. "Boss, how do ya figger we *are* gonna ketch him?"

The tall, blond owner of the Broken Wheel looked at his foreman and winked. "Don't give up the ship, Pete. I've got a plan. What's more, it might work."

Pete looked relieved. "What is it?"

"I'll tell you all about it after I've worked out the details." Jim grew businesslike. "But I'll say this right now—standing around shooting the breeze is no way to run a horse ranch." He turned to his visitor. "How about staying for a bite of lunch, Charlie?"

"Don't mind if I do. I understand Pete here is the finest food wrangler this side of Paris, France."

"Aw, come on now," Pete drawled, blushing through his tan.

"What're you going to rustle up for us?" Jim asked.

"Wal, lemme see. How'd you fellas feel about a mess of barbecued spareribs?"

"Sounds a lot better than plain dry bread," Stevens said.

Jim started down the porch steps. "Come on, Charlie. While Pete's burning the ribs, I'll take you out and introduce you to your new mares."

"Right."

Pete shouted after them. "Lissen—I ain't gonna stand over a hot bed of charcoal fer nothin'. So when the ribs are ready to eat, I'll shoot off a cannon, an' I expect you fellers to come a-runnin'."

"I'll be at the table before the echo dies away," Stevens promised. "When it comes to barbecued spareribs, wild horses couldn't hold me back."

After lunch, Charlie Stevens ungreased his fingers on a damp napkin, pushed his chair back and regarded the platterful of well-gnawed ribs. "Speaking of wild horses—as I was before Pete summoned me to this midday banquet—it isn't often any more that we hear about mustang stallions roaming the ranges with wild herds. It sounds like a romantic throwback to the days of the Old West."

"It shore does," Pete agreed. "Many's the time I heered my pop an' gran'pop tell them yarns when me an' my brother was kids. Sometimes I think them old boys jest made up them stories to pass the long winter evenin's." Pete stared at the ceiling, looking back into his boyhood. "In them yarns they use'ta tell, the big mustang stallion was always milk-white, an' he had big, black eyes like lumps of coal. An' they always made him out to be like a spook horse. He was so fast an' so tricky, nobody could ever ketch him, no matter how dang hard they tried. He roamed the Texas ranges, back in the '70's. They even had a special fancy name fer him: 'The Ghost of the Staked Plain.' "

Stevens looked at Pete, deadpan. "Pete, are you sure this Fury isn't a ghost, too?"

The old foreman slammed his fist down so hard, the top layer of bare bones slid off the pile and clattered to the table. "Fury's no ghost, dang it! We seen him with our own eyes, didn't we, Jim?"

"Keep your shirt on," Jim said, smiling. "Charlie's only needling you a little."

"Then make him quit! It's nothin' to joke about! Why, Fury's—he's even *better'n* that ole white mustang! He's bigger—he's stronger—he's trickier—he's faster—he's—" Pete sputtered, his mouth flapping like a window shade in a high wind. For once the old horse-handler was at a loss for words.

Stevens reached out and clapped Pete on the back. "Look, oldtimer, I didn't mean to get you so riled-up. I didn't realize you were so much in love with this Fury of yours."

"Fergit it!" Pete snapped, reaching for the agate pot. "Here—have some more hot coffee—an' I hope it scalds yer gullet!"

Jim laughed. "You see, Charlie? When the subject is Fury, Pete isn't going to stand for any kidding." He held out his own cup to be filled. "But I assure you, Fury's no ghost."

"I'm beginning to believe you," Stevens admitted.

Jim went on: "You know something, Pete? Your pop and grandpop didn't make up those stories about the milk-white stallion. They merely repeated what they'd heard. The mustangers of the Old West had hundreds of legends about the swift, savage horses that refused to be captured. Every range had its own mysterious mustang. Up in the Pacific Northwest they used to tell about a steel-blue stallion with flint-colored eyes and a silver mane and tail."

"Is that right?" Pete said, fascinated. "Did they ever ketch him?"

"Nope. The way the story went, he roamed east to the Montana badlands and haunted the boys for years. Those legendary stallions never got caught. They just appeared on the horizon on moonlit nights, then faded into nowhere."

"No foolin'," Pete said, wide-eyed. "Them spooky critters musta drove the cowhands nigh crazy."

"Well," Stevens said, pushing his chair back, "I hope this Fury doesn't drive you two fellows crazy."

"No danger of that," Jim said. "Fury's no legendary animal—and he isn't going to get away from us. Right, Pete?"

"Right as rawhide!" Pete said.

That night, as Jim Newton sat with Pete before the crackling fire in the living room of the ranchhouse, he outlined his plan for capturing Fury. As the foreman listened, his eyes danced with excitement.

"Now," Jim said finally. "What's your opinion? Think it'll work?"

"Sure, it'll work. Why won't it?"

"Because its success depends on Fury himself. And from what you and I have seen, that wild stallion's every bit as cagey and smart as those mythical ghost-horses we were talking about this afternoon. We can bait the trap, Pete, but we can't be absolutely sure that such a clever horse will fall for it."

"That's right, we can't," Pete said, frowning. He reached into the fireplace and relit his pipe from the glowing end of a half-burned stick. After a few seconds he blew out a cloud of smoke and looked at his boss. "But we gotta try it, Jim—else that Charlie Stevens'll be up there in the hills, tryin' hisself. An' we can't let *him* git Fury—kin we?"

"We certainly can't. Fury belongs to us."

"Then it's all settled. When do we start?"

"Tomorrow morning at five," Jim said.

For many hours the two riders had been following a trail of fresh manure, without even catching a glimpse of a mustang. Finally, when the sun was directly overhead, they came upon a group of four mares who were grazing away from the main herd. Because they were separated from their leader, the animals were more inquisitive than frightened. Without moving their feet, they followed Jim and Pete with their heads as the men maneuvered their mounts to a position which cut off the mares' possible escape back to the herd. The rest of the operation was easy for Jim and Pete, because rounding up wild horses was the way they made their living. Whooping and waving their hats, they galloped toward the mustangs, who squealed and took flight ahead of the men.

Three hours later, the wild mares were safely inclosed in the main corral at the Broken Wheel. Fury had lost four members of his herd; and Jim and Pete hoped that he'd be curious enough to do something drastic about trying to get them back.

That night, long after darkness fell, Jim opened the west gate of the corral and took a position at one side of the opening. Pete took his own station at the far side. On the ground between them lay a length of rope. For the better part of an hour, neither man spoke a word or made a sound. Shortly after eleven, they heard the four wild mares inside the corral approaching the open gate, sniffing suspiciously. Then sud-

denly, sensing that the opening was the way back to
freedom on the range, they made a dash for it. At the
same instant, Jim and Pete raised the rope and lashed
it around the gate-posts. The startled mares slammed
into it, screamed with fright, and dashed back into
the inclosure, where they stood trembling in a tight
huddle.

The men lowered the rope to the ground again and
resumed their silent watch. An hour went by, then still
another. Finally the moon rose over the ranchhouse
behind them. Pete looked across at Jim and with raised
palms asked a silent question. Jim shrugged and motioned to Pete to move back into the shadow of the
gate-post. Both men longed for a smoke, knowing at
the same time that such a thing was impossible.
Through their minds raced the same painful thought
—that this joint-stiffening waiting might be all in
vain.

Finally, as the moon began its march, and the
meadow and the hills beyond were bathed in cold
light, they heard the mares nickering. Glancing back
into the corral, they saw the animals in silhouette. The
mares were no longer standing together; all were peering westward toward the range. Jim swung his head
around. Was something moving out there in the distance? Yes, it was—he was sure of it. He glanced at
Pete. Pete nodded vigorously; he had seen it, too. The
mares behind them nickered again and took a few
steps forward. Jim tugged lightly at the rope, and Pete
telegraphed the answer that he was ready.

The mares approached the gate again, timidly, halt-
ingly. Soft, excited gurglings came from their throats.
Presently, they made a concerted rush for the opening, but as the men lifted the rope the mares saw it
rise in the moonlight and retreated again in mad fright.
One of them raised her head and neighed hysterically.

From the lonely distance, at the far boundary of the meadow, came an answer—the full, deep-toned cry of a stallion!

With hearts pounding and breath quickening, the men lowered the rope to the ground and stared toward the silvered hills. Not four hundred yards away, they saw him coming! Fury—the ebony king of the range! He was moving at an easy gallop, his hoofs making hollow, drumlike sounds on the grass.

The mares keened softly, exploring the fence, excitedly seeking another way out but not daring again to approach the gate where they had twice been turned back by the fearsome rope.

Fury came forward in an arrow line, ears standing straight up; wide nostrils flaring; wild eyes reflecting the brilliant moon. Jim and Pete held the rope so taut on the ground that they could feel it cutting into their horny palms.

The stallion saw the opening in the fence and rushed at it in a straight, true line. Then abruptly, not ten yards away from the crouching men, he stopped and stood still. Jim and Pete looked up at the mighty animal, hardly daring to draw a breath. He flung his head back and sniffed the air. Inside the corral, the mares danced and whimpered, imploring him to join them.

Agonizing seconds dragged by, while the wary stallion held the men in painful suspense. And then— slowly and regally—Fury moved forward and crossed the rope.

Pete let out a whoop and slammed the corral gate. The startled stallion gave a shrill scream and rose to his hind legs, ready to do battle. He was a second too late—the trap had been sprung.

Fury—the jetblack stallion of the hills—now belonged to the Broken Wheel Ranch.

CHAPTER 2

Joey

EVERY SPRING, the picket fence around the Children's Home on the town square received a new coat of white paint. This year the chore was entrusted to Joey Clark. The superintendent of the institution, Mr. Taylor, knew that the boy would do a nice, neat job, because Joey was handy and liked any kind of work that could be done outdoors. Mr. Taylor also felt that if Joey were doing something he didn't mind doing, he would stay out of trouble. So two people were satisfied this bright Saturday morning—Joey and Mr. Taylor.

Joey dipped his brush into the can of white paint and started on the last picket next to the gate. When it was finished, he took a couple of steps backward and looked at the sections of the fence that he had completed. The up-and-down white boards reminded him of stripes on a zebra. Joey had seen a zebra the previous summer, when the circus had come to town and all the youngsters at the Children's Home had been invited. He had admired the zebra because it looked like a fancy horse, and any animal resembling a horse, or related to one, was okay with Joey, because the boy was what the other boys called horse-crazy.

As Joey gazed at the picket fence, he thought of the old riddle about zebras. Was a zebra a black horse with white stripes, or a white horse with black stripes?

It was an important question that nobody had ever settled. He set the paint can down, leaned on the gate, and thought about the problem for a few minutes. In his mind's eye, he pictured a small white horse and a small black horse. If he striped the white one with black paint and the black one with white paint, which one would look more like a zebra? Joey shook his head. In his mind, they both looked like zebras.

Joey was still pondering the question when Bud Harvey came along the sidewalk on his bike. Joey had always envied Bud, not only because Bud had a job delivering the newspaper all over town, but also because he had a father and a mother and lived with them in a nice little house.

Joey, at thirteen, couldn't remember living anywhere but in the Children's Home. But he often dreamed of what it would be like to live with his own folks, instead of with a superintendent and a bunch of other boys. He liked the other kids all right, and Mr. Taylor was a nice man—but he was kind of strict, not easygoing, as Joey imagined a boy's real father would be. Of course, Mr. Taylor had to be strict; he had seventeen boys to look out for. But sometimes Joey wished that the "super" would act more like a father—not punishing him all the time for getting out of line or for violating one or more of all those doggone rules and regulations of the Home.

Deep down inside, what Joey really yearned for was an honest-to-goodness father. As far as the boy knew, his parents, whoever they were or had been, were dead. But he often wondered what his father had been like. Joey knew exactly what he wanted him to be like. He'd be tall and slim, with skin that was bronzed by life in the open. And he'd have kind, blue eyes and a strong mouth with smile-wrinkles around it. This man that Joey wanted his father to be worked with horses somehow—maybe on a ranch. And just about now, when Joey was growing taller and stronger, his father would be giving him a horse of his own to ride and take care of. A horse of his own! Boy, Joey thought, wouldn't that be something!

In his daydreams, Joey lived with that wonderful horse every minute—training him, grooming him, riding him. He would be the greatest horse in the whole West, and people would ride in from miles around just to see him and admire him. That horse of yours—they'd say to Joey—there's a real animal!

But now, in reality, it was Saturday morning at the Home, and Joey's mind was working on the zebra riddle. And here was Bud Harvey on his bike. The wire basket on the handlebars was stuffed with copies of *The Valley Mirror,* the weekly newspaper. Bud braked his bike and grabbed hold of the gate to steady himself.

"Hi, Joey."

Joey came out of his trance. "Oh, hi, Bud."

"What're you doing?"

"Painting the fence. What's it look like?"

Bud laughed. "Looks like you're goldbricking. You were leaning on the gate, just staring."

Joey felt a little embarrassed. "Oh—I was thinking about something, before getting started on the gate."

"Thinking about what—horses?" Bud grinned. He'd heard about Joey being called horse-crazy.

Joey didn't want to admit that he'd been trying to solve the zebra riddle—it would be too tough to explain. So he said, "Sure, Bud, that's right. I was thinking about horses."

"Boy," Bud said, "that's all you ever think about. What do you get to eat in this place, oats?"

"Yeah," Joey said sharply, "oats. That's all we ever

get. Mr. Taylor feeds 'em to us three times a day, in nosebags."

"Gosh, you don't have to get sore," Bud said. "I was only kidding." He handed Joey a copy of the *Mirror*. "Here's Mr. Taylor's paper. Don't get it full of paint before he sees it, or he'll flip his lid."

Joey didn't answer. His eyes were glued to a picture at the bottom of the front page. It was a photograph of a black stallion. His name was under it in capital letters—FURY.

"Oh, boy!" Joey muttered. "Holy mackerel!"

Bud squinted. "What is it?"

Joey held up the paper and pointed to the picture.

"Oh, yeah," Bud said. "That's some horse."

"Horse? He's a wild *stallion!"*

"Okay, so he's a wild stallion. It tells all about him there. Some ranchers captured him a couple days ago." Bud shoved his bike away from the gate and began pedaling. "See ya, Joey," he called back. "I gotta get these papers delivered. My dad's taking me to the rodeo this afternoon."

Joey didn't even notice that Bud was gone. He sat on the grass, eagerly reading the story that went with the picture. It told about a young rancher named Jim Newton and his foreman Pete. They had a spread in the valley called the Broken Wheel. It described how they had discovered a wild stallion guarding a herd and how they had named him Fury and lured him down from the hills, and the way they had corralled him in the dead of night.

As Joey read the story, it wasn't Jim and Pete who crouched in the shadow of the corral—it was Joey Clark. It was Joey who waited with pounding heart as the stallion hesitated, then crossed the rope. It was Joey who let out a whoop and slammed the gate on the captured animal.

He gazed longingly at Fury's picture, riding a cloud of imagination. A sharp tap on the shoulder brought him back to earth with a crash. He looked up, gulped, and scrambled to his feet. It was Mr. Taylor, the superintendent.

Mr. Taylor had a faceful of storm warnings. "For heaven's sake, Joey," he began, "can't you ever be trusted to finish a job?"

"But, Mr. Taylor—" Joey began.

"Joey, when the work assignments were made this morning, this painting job was the one you asked for. I gave it to you because I thought you'd do it well."

"I was just about to start on the gate," Joey faltered.

"The gate should be finished by this time. All the other boys have almost completed their assignments. But what do I find you doing? I find you sitting on the ground, reading the comics in the paper."

"I wasn't reading the comics," Joey protested. "I was reading about Fury."

"About what?"

"Fury. He's a wild stallion."

"Oh, no!" said Mr. Taylor, rolling his eyes upward. "Not horses! Not *again!*"

"But, sir," Joey said. "Fury isn't just an ordinary horse. You don't understand. He's a wild stallion!"

Mr. Taylor sighed and shook his head. A wild stallion, he thought. What makes this boy imagine I don't understand wild stallions? I have seventeen of them under my care, and this boy Joey Clark is the wildest of them all.

The superintendent wasn't a cruel or a thoughtless man; he was actually a kindly person, dedicated to the care of homeless boys.

Bringing up even one boy presents certain problems, but Mr. Taylor's problems were multiplied by seventeen. Actually by eighteen—because Joey Clark was twice as hard to handle as any other one boy the man had ever had in his charge.

Joey wasn't a bad boy; he was just headstrong and wilful. He liked having his own way about almost everything, and that made him troublesome. Mr. Taylor liked Joey but knew that what the boy needed was constant, individual supervision and expert training, as did this wild stallion in the newspaper. Unfortunately, with sixteen other boys in the house, Mr. Taylor didn't have the time to give Joey constant personal attention. That was a father's job—and this poor boy didn't have a father.

The harassed superintendent sighed again. The other boys had finished their chores and had started a ball game in the yard behind the main house. He and Joey could hear the yelling and the thud of balls in gloves. But there was such a thing as discipline, and besides, the painting job had to be finished.

"Sorry, Joey," Mr. Taylor said regretfully. "No ball-playing till you finish your assignment."

Joey looked the man squarely in the eye for a moment, then picked up the brush and the can of paint without a word and began to slap the paint on the gate.

"Neatly," Mr. Taylor warned. "If it isn't done neatly, you'll have to do it over."

Joey didn't answer. Shaking his head wearily, the superintendent gathered the windblown sheets of the newspaper together and made his way back to the house.

The paint ran out when the gate was about two-thirds finished, and Joey had to go inside to get a new can. When the job was finally completed, it was eleven-thirty. Joey hadn't really missed playing ball with the other kids, because while painting he relived the exciting newspaper story about the capture of Fury. Now his mind started buzzing with plans and questions. First of all, he knew he just had to see this famous wild stallion with his own eyes. How could he arrange it? Could he get Mr. Taylor to drive him out to the Broken Wheel Ranch someday soon? That didn't seem likely. If Joey went, all the other kids would have to go, too, and the institution had no bus. It seemed like an unbeatable problem, but Joey was determined that he was going to see Fury. He'd get out to the ranch somehow, even if he had to break rule number one and leave the Home without permission. The army had a word for this crime—AWOL. Joey decided that he wouldn't mind being punished for going AWOL if it enabled him to meet Fury.

Presently, as he stepped back from the gate to look for any spots that his paintbrush might have missed, his ears caught the magnificent sound of a brass band. He realized immediately what it was—the rodeo parade. While thinking about Fury, he had forgotten that the parade was scheduled to come through town that morning. The rodeo was to take place during the afternoon at the Fairgrounds, and the contestants were riding through the streets as an advertisement.

Anxious to see the parade, the other sixteen boys came galloping and whooping across the lawn toward the freshly painted fence.

"Hey, watch it—the paint's wet!" Joey warned. As he gestured toward the fence, he almost dropped the can of paint but got a grip on the handle just in time.

The chattering boys lined up as closely as possible to the glistening white pickets. Naturally, every one of them had to test the paint with a finger to see if it really was as wet as Joey had said. It was—and each boy now had a white fingertip.

Mr. Taylor came hurrying across the lawn, shouting, "Don't wipe it on your dungarees, boys!" But of course he spoke too late. A man has to talk fast when sixteen excited boys have wet paint on their fingers.

By this time the parade had swung around the corner and was approaching the grounds of the Children's Home. The band was playing "Deep in the Heart of Texas." The musicians were cowboys wearing wide leather chaps, bright-colored shirts and ten-gallon hats. Their leader was a cowgirl with long golden hair. She wore a short green skirt and high white leather boots with red tassels, and twirled a "diamond"-studded baton that sparkled in the sunlight. As the band marched past the fence, the boys shouted and waved, and the beautiful drum majorette smiled and waved back. Then she threw her baton high into the air and caught it just before it hit the ground. The delighted boys clapped their hands and cheered.

All at once the band was forgotten. And no wonder —for immediately behind it rode the rodeo contestants, a long line of cowboys and cowgirls with tanned faces. Some of the men had their lariats out, roping pretty girls who stood on the sidewalk. The clop-clop of the horses' hoofs on the asphalt brought more cheers from the boys but sent cold shivers down Joey's spine. He had never seen so many horses all in one place, not even at the circus the year before. Certainly, he'd never been so close to fine cow ponies, and as he watched them he felt a sudden impulse to get even closer. With the handle of his paintbrush he quietly slid back the bolt of the gate.

Mr. Taylor had been keeping one suspicious eye on Joey. There were scores of horses right there in front of the Home, and, as all the boys said, Joey was horse-crazy, so Mr. Taylor was on the alert. Seeing Joey slide the bolt and push the gate open, he called a sharp command to him: "Joey—stay here!"

Joey paid no attention to Mr. Taylor but dashed out through the gate and across the sidewalk.

"Joey! Come back inside the fence!"

The boy didn't even hear the order, for by that time he was in the street, in the very middle of the parade, gleefully waving his brush with one hand and holding the can of paint with the other. In his haste to get close to the horses, he hadn't even thought to leave the can inside the gate.

As Joey stood gaping at a dapper pinto pony, one of the cowboys who had been roping the parade-watchers picked Joey as his next victim. Just as he was getting his loop ready, a large open car trailing behind the pinto arrived at the spot where Joey stood. An important-looking man, seated in the back of the car, smiled and waved his ten-gallon hat. Joey looked at the man, not knowing that he was Mr. Cooper, mayor of the town. The cowboy with the rope made two swings over his head and shot the loop out to-ward Joey. At the last second, Joey saw it coming and instinctively flung his arms up to fend it off. The can of paint slipped from his fingers, sailed through the air into the car, and struck the mayor on the shoulder. The crowds on the sidewalk gasped as the startled dignitary lowered his head and helplessly watched the thick, white paint flow down over his blue suit into his lap.

For a second or two, the onlookers were shocked into silence; then a great peal of laughter went up all along the block. At first, Joey was unaware of what had happened, for he was trying to loosen the rope that encircled his waist. But when he looked up and saw the enraged, paint-covered mayor, he realized that he had been the cause of the disaster, and he turned cold from head to foot.

The driver of the car turned the wheel sharply and pulled in to the curb. The dripping mayor stood up in the back seat, shook his finger at Joey, and loudly demanded satisfaction. Mr. Taylor, his face as white as the paint on the mayor's suit, rushed to the other side of the car, sputtering apologies.

Joey's first terrified impulse was to escape from the scene. He actually did try to run, but the cowboy who had roped him was pulling him in like a fish on a line. With the exception of the mayor, Mr. Taylor and Joey, everybody was roaring with laughter.

Mr. Taylor dashed from the side of the mayor's car, grabbed Joey roughly by the arm, and began to give him a tongue lashing that would have won first prize in a mule-skinner's contest. The cowboy leaned down from his saddle and loosened the rope, then pulled the loop up over Joey's head.

"I reckon this here is yore fish, mister," he said to Mr. Taylor. He chuckled and patted Joey on the head. "Sonny," he drawled, "next time I hear that cowboy song about saddlin' ole Paint, I'll thank you fer givin' it a brand-new meanin'." With a wink at Joey he galloped off to join the parade.

Mr. Taylor took a firm hold on Joey's wrist and dragged him in the direction of the mayor's car. Just before they reached it, the mayor gave a sharp order to his driver, and the car pulled away. The unfortunate man wanted nothing quite so much as a turpentine bath and a clean suit of clothes.

Mr. Taylor prodded Joey through the gate. "You go up to your dormitory and stay there!" he commanded. "You're not to come out, understand?"

Joey nodded glumly, feeling that the accident to the

mayor had not been entirely his fault. He considered himself the victim of circumstances beyond his control and didn't think he should be punished. As Joey walked toward the house, Mr. Taylor called after him.

"No movie for you tonight! You're going to stay in the dorm till tomorrow morning at church time!"

Joey didn't care about missing the evening movie, but the order about staying in the dorm all day came as a shock. The rodeo was scheduled for that afternoon, and, having seen part of the parade, Joey wanted to go. Suddenly, he felt belligerent. Nothing was going to keep him from going to the rodeo, not even the thought of the punishment that would surely follow his breaking the rules.

He pranced through the front door of the Home, continued straight down the hall, and went right out the back door, unseen by anybody. Ten minutes later he was standing on Main Street, trying to hitch a ride to the Fairgrounds.

CHAPTER 3

Rodeo Day

THE EXCITEMENT of Rodeo Day lit a firecracker under almost everybody in that part of the state. All the stores in town had signs in the windows, announcing that they were closing on the dot of noon. Housewives did their shopping early in the morning, while their husbands went to the bank to draw out extra cash to spend at the Fairgrounds. The youngsters bounded out of bed as soon as it was daylight, and came down to breakfast wearing their cowboy suits and gun belts. When they went to the grocery store with their mothers, they ducked behind shelves of cereal boxes and canned goods and practiced quick-drawing on other youngsters who came in. Cap pistols cracked without a letup, and small gun-toters dropped to the floor clutching their chests, as though shot straight through the heart. Everybody took these bloody battles good-naturedly except Mr. Gansemeyer, the manager of the supermarket, who finally broke under the strain. When the Farley twins knocked over a tall pyramid of canned soup while engaged in a six-gun showdown, Mr. Gansemeyer chased them out and stationed a clerk at the front door to bar all small fry who carried weapons.

It wasn't only the dudes in town who had rodeo fever that Saturday morning. Even the real horsemen and cowmen in the valley were stricken with it. At the

Broken Wheel Ranch, Jim Newton and Pete rolled out early to get a whole day's chores done by noon. Pete prepared a quick lunch, and they ate it standing up in the kitchen. Afterward, Pete washed the dishes hurriedly, because he wanted to get dressed in a fancy new outfit before leaving for town.

Jim put on a clean shirt and ranch pants, then walked out to the corrals to give the horses a once-over, and to leave some last minute instructions with Bart and Hank, his two bronc-busters. The stock in the big corral seemed happy and contented, so Jim moved along to the smaller one to have a look at Fury. The untamed stallion hadn't calmed down noticeably since his capture. He pranced nervously up and down the far side of the inclosure, wheeling quickly each time he reached a corner post. Jim noticed that Fury never took his angry eyes off Bart and Hank who were perched on the top rail of the near fence with their legs outside, ready to hop down in case the stallion took it into his head to charge over and make a lunge at them.

The two bronc-peelers had their heads turned toward Fury and didn't see Jim Newton approaching. Jim caught the tail end of something Bart was telling Hank:

". . . so one-a these days I'm gonna take a club to that ornery black devil, whether Newton likes it or not."

"That's the day you get tossed off this ranch!" Jim snapped.

Bart and Hank jerked their heads around and jumped down off the fence. Hank recognized anger in Jim's voice, and darted a glance at Bart. Bart's flabby, unpleasant face was as red as fire.

"What's the idea of sneakin' up on us?" he growled.

"I never sneak up on anybody," Jim replied, in a

calm voice. "It's not my way." He looked straight at Bart. "Bart, I don't like what I just heard you say."

"If ya hadn't snuck up like an Indian ya wouldn'ta heard it," Bart muttered.

"But I'm glad I did hear it, because now I can give you my final word, and it's this: Any man on the ranch who uses rough tactics on my horses gets half an hour to pack his bedroll and high-tail it out of here." Jim paused. "You got that straight?"

Bart gave a surly nod and spat on the ground.

Jim turned to Hank. "You savvy it, too?"

Hank grinned. "Sure, Jim. . . . Look—Bart didn't mean what he just said. He's just a mite sizzled 'cause Fury come at him a couple minutes ago with his ears laid back and his teeth showin'."

"How'd that happen, Bart?" Jim asked. "Did you go inside the corral?"

"Sure I did. It's my job to break horses, ain't it? Ain't that what I git paid for?"

"Certainly, but don't forget—a mustang stallion's just about the wildest animal alive, and could kill you easily. You can't tame Fury by beating him. He's got to be broken gently or he can be ruined."

Bart curled his lip. "You don't hafta tell me that, I'm no greenhorn. I just tried to slip a hackamore on him, that's all. Then he made like to paw me. Almost chopped me down with them hoofs-a his."

"Well, take it in easy steps," Jim said, cooling off a little. "Fury'll make a good mount, once he's broken to ride. But it can't be done in a day or even a week. Okay?"

Bart shrugged. "You're the boss."

Bart was a drifter, moving from job to job, but Jim had hired him recently because the man had wrangled for some very good outfits. Bart was about thirty-five, dark-bearded and stubby, and inclined to be a bit overweight, but he knew horses. The trouble was, he didn't know men very well. In addition, he had a short, evil temper.

Hank, on the other hand, was quiet and easygoing, with twinkling eyes and a quick sense of humor. He'd busted broncs for Jim for a long time and was a good man to have around. Everybody liked Hank, and once he'd checked in at a ranch that suited him he never thought much about drifting. Slow to take offense, he even got along with Bart, despite Bart's chip-on-the-shoulder attitude. Hank admired good ropers more than anything else, and Bart could cast a loop as well as any buster Hank had ever come across.

"Well, boys," Jim said, "that's that. Pete and I are driving into town."

Hank looked Jim up and down and smiled. "I took notice you were all slicked up. Goin' to the rodeo?"

"That's right. You men can take it easy this afternoon. If you feel like it maybe you can try to gentle Fury down—from a safe distance. Talk to him a little. Try to get him used to the human voice."

"So far that critter don't seem to think too much of the human voice," Hank said. "Lookit him out there, Jim. He's givin' us the evil eye for sure."

The three men looked toward Fury, who had stopped prancing and was trying to stare them down.

Bart cupped his hands and shouted, "Hey, there, wild hoss! *Hey!*" He climbed up onto the bottom rail and leaned into the corral. "Hey, killer—come over here!"

Fury folded his ears back and bannered his tail. The men watched in silence. Suddenly, the horse charged toward the fence. Bart stayed on the rail until Fury was five yards away, then he jumped back to safety in a big hurry. Two seconds before he would have slammed into the fence, the horse jammed his forefeet into the ground, raised his head at Bart and bawled his rage.

Bart shook a hairy fist. "Go ahead and holler your fool head off! You'll soon find out who's boss!"

From deep down in his chest Fury let out a noisy blast of air, spun around, and raced back to the far side of the corral. Jim and Hank laughed.

"He sure told you off, Bart," Hank said. "That was the biggest razzberry I ever heard a horse blow."

Bart's face turned scarlet. He glared at Hank and was about to say something, but instead he spat into the corral and slouched off toward the bunkhouse.

Jim wrinkled his brow but said nothing until Bart had disappeared. "Hank, that man's looking for trouble, and he'll find it if he doesn't cool off. Keep a weather eye out while we're gone, will you? And for gosh sakes don't let Bart set foot inside Fury's corral."

Hank winked knowingly. "Don't worry, Jim, I'll take care of things. You and Pete get goin' and have yourselves a good rodeo."

"Thanks," Jim said. He clapped Hank on the shoulder and walked back toward the house. "Hey, Pete, come on!" he shouted. "Quit smearing your hair with goose grease and let's move!"

The door of the ranchhouse opened, and old Pete came down the porch steps dressed in a new pair of levis, a green silk shirt with a red neckerchief, a white ten-gallon hat, and custom-made yellow boots with two-inch heels.

Jim widened his eyes in mock surprise and gave a wolf-whistle. "Well, blow me down! If it isn't a movie star!"

"Aw, go soak yer head!" Pete muttered, self-consciously. "A man oughta look his best at the rodeo, oughtn't he?"

"That's right," Jim said, chuckling. "And you look

like a cowgirl's dream. Come on, dude, let's get roll-ing."

A moment later, Jim Newton and his foreman were headed for town in the station wagon with the name *Broken Wheel Ranch* painted on its side doors.

After Joey left the back door of the Children's Home, it didn't take him long to get a hitch to the Fairgrounds. Two college boys picked him up in their hotrod and gave him the wildest ride he'd ever had. Joey sat in the back seat with his heart in his throat, as the souped-up jalopy skinned in and out of the heavy traffic. When they arrived at the main gate, Joey was pale with fright. He wasn't sorry to set his feet on the ground again with all his bones intact. After he'd thanked the boys for the lift, he watched them roar off in a cloud of blue smoke to find a park-ing place.

Joey had never seen so many people in one place in his life. It looked as though everybody in fourteen counties was at the Fairgrounds, all trying to jam through the ticket gate at the same time. There were whole families in the crowd; youngsters pleading for hotdogs and popcorn, and a few mothers calling for small children who had become lost or separated from them. Butchers, bakers, plumbers and bankers rubbed elbows with dude ranchers and honest-to-goodness cowmen. Joey saw one little boy, who couldn't have been more than two years old, dressed like a cowboy, with a pair of six-shooters in holsters that hung all the way down to his tiny boots. Joey laughed when he noticed that the young wrangler held onto his mother's hand in a most uncowboylike fashion.

It wasn't until Joey smelled the tantalizing odor of broiling meat that he remembered he hadn't had a bite to eat since breakfast. But when he put his hands in the pockets of his dungarees he received a shock—he hadn't any money. In his locker he had eight dollars and forty-seven cents, but in his haste to escape, it hadn't occurred to him to rush upstairs and get it. Now he was faced with a real problem—how to get into the Fairgrounds without money for a ticket.

While Joey's mind pondered this question, his nose led him to the source of the delicious odor. He could see hundreds of people swarming around a huge fire, and other folks wearing happy expressions were emerging from the swarm, gnawing on meatpacked sandwiches made with giant, golden rolls. Joey spoke to a tall boy who was eating one sandwich and holding another.

"Hey, what do they charge for those things?"

"Nothin', they're free," the boy said, biting off a large piece of pink, juicy meat. "Better get in there," he mumbled.

"Yeah, I guess I better. Look—how come it's free?"

" 'Cause it is." The boy motioned to a sign. "Read what it says."

Joey stood on tiptoe and read the sign: COME ONE—COME ALL! FREE BARBECUE! DONATED BY RANCH OWNERS OF LINCOLN COUNTY!

Joey's mouth was watering, "Gee whiz!" he exclaimed. When he turned to say thanks, the boy had disappeared. Joey elbowed his way through the crowd and finally managed to get close to the spot where a group of men and women were forking chunks of meat off the fire, slapping them into rolls, and cheerfully giving them out to the scores of outstretched hands. Big pits dug in the ground held the beds of glowing coals. The meat was broiling on net wire spread across the pits. After a struggle to get served, Joey was handed a barbecue sandwich by a tall, smiling man, who said, "Enjoy it, sonny."

"Thank you, sir," Joey said, grinning back at the man. A minute later, the barbecue sauce was dripping from the sandwich and running up Joey's arm, as he looked around for a place where he could stand and eat without being trampled on.

After he'd finished, he wiped his hands on the grass and pushed through the crowd around the outside of the grandstand. He smelled the hotdogs and the hamburgers, but he was no longer hungry. There were more people now; they were coming from every direction. The tension of the rodeo was mounting higher every minute. Many people were dressed in dude outfits, each costume a little gaudier than the next. Real cowboys, too, rangy, brown-faced men, hung around outside before going in to compete in the contests.

Joey still hadn't figured out a way to get inside without a ticket, so he kept walking close to the fence looking at the ground, hoping to find a ticket that somebody had lost, but he had no luck. The rodeo was scheduled to start in about half an hour, and he still didn't know how he was going to get past the ticket taker. By the time he reached the far side of the fence, away from the dense crowds, he felt terribly depressed.

As he walked with his head down, he almost tripped over a pair of long legs stretched out on the ground. They belonged to a cowboy who was sitting in the grass. His back rested against the fence, and his wide-brimmed hat was pulled down over his forehead to shade his eyes from the sun. He seemed to be asleep. His face was leathery and sun browned and covered with a red stubble. He had on a pair of bullhide batwing chaps over faded levis. Joey stared at the dozing man with envy, sensing that he was a genuine cowpuncher. As the boy watched, the man opened one pale blue eye and flashed a smile. Two front teeth of his upper jaw were missing, and Joey couldn't help looking at the vacant space where the teeth should have been.

"I reckon yore wonderin' how I can bite into an apple," the man drawled.

Joey flushed with embarrassment. "Oh, no, sir. I just couldn't help noticing."

"Ain't no charge for lookin'. Them two teeth was knocked clean out by a calf when I was tyin' him." The cowboy pushed his hat back. "You've heered tell about the wide open spaces? Wal—that's what I got right here in mah mouth—wide open spaces." The man laughed so hard, Joey couldn't help laughing, too.

"Are you gonna be in the rodeo?" Joey asked.

"I am, shore 'nuff. That's why I'm back here takin' a snooze. A beauty sleep before gittin' bounced by a bronc always kinda helps to calm me down." The cowboy took a sack of tobacco and a piece of paper from his shirt pocket and rolled a smoke with one hand. After the cigarette was licked and lighted he put out his hand. "Mah name's Red Sweeny, what's yore's?"

"Joey Clark." Red's hand felt strong and calloused.

"What're you doin' here on this side of the grandstand, Joey? The ticket gate's around yonder."

"I know, but I haven't got a ticket. I thought maybe I'd find one that somebody lost."

Red snorted. "Fat chance. Nobody *never* loses a rodeo ticket. Ain't you got no money?"

"Oh, sure," Joey said hastily. "I've got eight dollars and forty-seven cents, only not with me. I left it back at the Home—I mean back at my house."

"Rough goin'." Red took out a ragged wallet, turned it upside down and shook it. "I'd shore like to stake ya, Joey, but like you see here, I'm flat busted."

"Gosh, that's awful nice of you, Red, but I—"

Red cut in, "I come up from Texas with fifty-five beautiful, hard-earned bucks. But the entry fees like to cleaned me out. Cost me twenty-five fer saddle bronc-ridin', a double sawbuck fer bulldoggin', an' an extry ten to help mah pardner in the wild-hoss race." He chuckled. "So looks like I jest gotta do some winnin' today, or me an' mah stummick'll be on nasty terms with one another."

"Gee, I sure hope you do win," Joey said.

"Much obliged." Red frowned. "Joey, how do you figger on gittin' into the rodeo?"

"I don't know, Red." He kicked the ground, violently. "But I gotta get in! I just *got* to!"

"Whatta ya mean you *got* to?"

"Well—it's kinda hard to explain. I've never seen a rodeo in my whole life, and I love horses more than anything, and—well—I've got to get in, that's all!" Joey was on the verge of tears.

Red reached up and took hold of Joey's arm. "Hey, ease off a little. No cause to feel that bad on account-a one lil ole ticket. Anybody feels like you do about horses can't miss a rodeo. So let's do some figgerin'." He studied Joey's troubled face. "Joey, how much nerve you got?"

"What do you mean?"

"Wal, I was jest thinkin'. If I was a boy that liked hosses—an' I had nerve enough—I'd git in that line at the gate an' shoot right past that ole ticket taker."

Joey opened his eyes wide. "But—suppose I get caught."

Red winked. "On the other hand, suppose you don't. Look on the bright side." He cocked his head and looked righteous. "Look, Joey, mebbe what I'm suggestin' ain't exactly honest. But in a emergency like this—you bein' a hoss-lover—maybe the good Lord'll understand an' forgive." Red got off the ground slowly and stretched his lanky frame. "Wal, I got to go in an' find me a mount fer the Grand Entry. An' later on, when I come buckin' outa that bronc chute, I expect you to be in there, a-cheerin' for me. Okay, Joey?"

"Okay, Red." Joey held out his hand, and Red shook it. "Good luck."

"Same to you—pardner."

They grinned at each other, then Red turned and headed for the contestants' gate. Joey watched the receding, bow-legged figure for a minute, then ran in the opposite direction. In his mind he could still hear Red's question: "Joey, how much nerve you got?" Well, Joey thought—I'll find that out in just a couple of minutes.

CHAPTER 4

The Rodeo

JIM NEWTON and Pete left the station wagon on the parking field and joined the crowd that was moving slowly toward the jammed ticket gate. There was a great deal of jostling and pushing, but everybody was good-humored about it except Pete, who grumbled because his new yellow boots were being trampled on. Finally, even Pete was mellowed by the tension and excitement of the occasion, and stopped growling, "Watch where yer goin', dang it!" every time his precious footwear was scuffed.

The two men met scores of old friends in the crowd, and nearly all of them had read the newspaper story about Fury's capture. Jim and Pete received congratulations at least a hundred times and even took some teasing about the danger of having a wild stallion on the Broken Wheel Ranch. Doc Weathers, the veterinarian, warned them that it was like having a tiger by the tail—they didn't dare hold on and didn't dare let go. Jim and Pete laughed. They couldn't help feeling a little proud of their unaccustomed fame.

Soon after they passed the carnival booths, they joined the single line filing through the entrance. They had bought reserved seats down in the front row, right next to the bronc chutes. When they'd moved to within ten feet of the gate, they noticed a boy standing on the grass watching the line. He wore a T-shirt and blue dungarees spotted with white paint. There was a wild, almost frightened look in his eyes, as though he wanted to do something desperate but couldn't find the courage.

Pete, who was in front of Jim in the line, nudged Jim in the stomach with his elbow and jerked a thumb toward the boy. "Lookit that kid there," he said over his shoulder. "Whatta ya reckon he's up to?"

Jim glanced at the boy again. "Maybe he's not up to anything. He might be just waiting for somebody."

Pete snorted. "Ya don't gulp that hard when yer just waitin' fer somebody."

Jim studied the boy's anxious face and felt inclined to agree. The boy was now inching toward the gate, watching the ticket taker warily. Jim and Pete each held their own tickets, and as they arrived at the entrance, they forgot about the boy. Pete handed his ticket over and took the torn-off stub, and at that moment somebody ran into him from behind, stepped on his foot, and almost knocked him down. From the edge of his eye he saw a small figure dart between himself and the ticket man. It was the boy in the T-shirt and blue dungarees.

"Hey!" the ticket man shouted. "Come back here!"

Pete swung around to Jim in a rage, pointing to a skinned mark on his left boot. "Look what that kid done! I *knowed* he was up to something!"

By that time the entrance was in an uproar. The ticket man shouted for one of the special guards, who lumbered off in pursuit of the fleeing boy. Some of the people in line, and those who had already passed through the gate, kept shouting encouragement at the boy.

The guard, who had a fat paunch, was no match for the boy's youth and speed. Within a few seconds

Joey had disappeared into the crowd under the grandstand. He had made it all right—he'd had just enough nerve.

Jim Newton, who had been left standing with his ticket in his hand, now gave it to the furious gateman. That boy's sure a wild one—Jim thought to himself. Then he half-smiled—for Jim was a man who had a great deal of sympathy for wild ones.

After Joey reached the grandstand, he kept a sharp lookout for the guard who had chased him. He didn't try to find an empty seat, because he wanted to move around and see everything that was going on. The rows of seats were crowded with people carrying pillows and lunch baskets, and everybody was laughing and shouting.

After ten minutes had gone by, Joey stopped worrying about the guard and gave his complete attention to a pre-rodeo cow pony race that was then lining up on the straight track. The riders had some trouble getting their horses properly strung out at the rope, but finally the starter fired his gun, and the horses took off down the straightaway. When the race was over, Joey didn't know or care who had won—it had been a beautiful thing to watch. He climbed over seats and scampered up and down aisles, and finally came to the stock pens, where dust-covered men were driving in the bulldogging steer. One of the sweating steermen told Joey that the steer were Brahmans; that they weighed about 1200 pounds; and that they could buck like horned hurricanes. Meanwhile, the drivers were shouting, the steer were bawling, and men with badges were calling out orders. Joey had never seen or heard anything like the excitement. He was riding on a cloud.

In the arena the dust swirled up in sharp gusts, but the water truck soon drove out to wet it down. Joey

watched this procedure for a few minutes, then moved
on to look for the bucking horses. He finally found them
in the bronc pen. They weren't bucking at the moment; they were simply standing quietly in the sun, with
nothing to worry about but flies. Joey looked down on
them and thought of Red Sweeny, knowing that Red
would be riding one of the four-legged jumping jacks
before the day was over.

The brassy call of a bugle brought Joey tearing
back into the grandstand. The gate at the far end of
the arena was flung open, and the Grand Entry began.
First came the brass band, followed by the flagbearers,
and everybody stood up and cheered as the Stars and
Stripes whipped past the stands. The contestants rode
behind the flags, and after they had gone one lap
around the track, they lined up in front of the grandstand. The announcer on the loudspeaker welcomed
one and all to the rodeo. He then introduced the governor, who stood up in the center box and waved to
the crowd. Introductions of other distinguished citi-
zens followed: guests from outside of the state and
leading contestants. At last the announcer said, "That's
it, folks—enjoy the rodeo!" Cheered by the people
in the stands, the parade line broke and the contestants galloped off whooping and waving their hats.

The first event to be announced was bareback steer
riding. When their names were called, the four judges
mounted on palominos rode out onto the field. Joey
gasped when he saw the golden animals with their
ivory manes and tails. He'd never realized that there
were such beautiful horses in the world.

He saw the big steer being pushed into the chutes,
and he ran down the aisle steps to the front rail, to
be as close as possible. In the first chute, a grim-
faced cowboy straddled the sideboards, ready for his
ride. The loud buzzing of the crowd stopped sud-

denly, and the silence that followed almost hurt Joey's ears. Every eye was on the chute, waiting for the first action of the rodeo. After an agonizing few seconds, the rider dropped down on the steer, and the gate swung open.

The announcer roared: "Chick Harper, coming out of chute one on steer seven!" The steer shot out like a truck bouncing along a rough road. Harper hung on for five jumps, then hit the dirt on his back and rolled away to avoid the pounding, bonebreaking hoofs. The people cheered as the officials drove the steer off the field.

Before the last steer came out, Joey saw the bronc men pushing the horses into the chutes. The boards clattered and boomed, as the nervous animals kicked their heels against them. But when the saddling began, the broncs quieted down and made no trouble. Meanwhile, the calf-roping was taking place, but Joey paid little attention; he was too fascinated by the activity among the saddle broncs. Suddenly he spied Red Sweeny in the second chute.

"Hey, Red!" he called excitedly. "Red! It's me— Joey!"

Red looked up, grinned, and returned to his saddling.

"Good luck, Red!" Joey shouted.

The busy cowboy waved one hand, without raising his head.

Jim Newton and Pete were seated in the first row, alongside the bronc chutes. When they heard Joey shouting at Red, they looked around.

"Hey, there's that ornery kid," Pete growled.

"Yes," Jim grinned. "The boy that gouged your new boots."

"It's nothin' to laugh at, dang it!" Pete pursed his

lips. "I'd sure like to give that kid a piece of my mind."

"Better hold on to those pieces," Jim needled. "You haven't got too many to spare."

"Ha-ha, big joke." Pete leaned down and rubbed the mark on his boot. Jim heard him mumbling to himself.

"I know one thing about that boy," Jim said. "He's crazy about horses. Get that expression on his face, Pete. He's looking at those broncs as if he loved them. For two bits I bet he'd fork one of them and ride."

"I wish he would," Pete snapped. "He'd be tossed so high he wouldn't come down for a week."

Jim shook his head. "Come on, Pete, cool down. Horses are more important than yellow boots and you know it."

"Okay, okay, let's fergit it," Pete said sourly. "The bronc ride's comin' up in a minute."

When the calf-roping event was over, the broncs were announced. Joey leaned over the rail and watched tensely as the gate cracked open and the first rider burst out. The man stayed aboard until the gun was fired, and received an ovation from the crowd.

It was Red Sweeny's turn now, and Joey felt his heart thumping. Red was straddling the chute, ready to drop down into the saddle. Joey was so excited that he didn't hear the clomp of heavy boots coming down the steps behind him. He had his attention glued to Red, who was scanning the arena, checking the position of his pickup men. At that moment of suspense and excitement—the blow fell. A heavy hand clamped down on Joey's shoulder. Startled, he jerked his head around and looked squarely into the angry, puffy face of the guard who had tried to catch him at the ticket gate.

"Caughtcha!" the guard yelled.

Joey's jaw fell, and he began to struggle.

"Stand still, kid!" the fat man growled. "I'm toss-in' you outa here!"

"No!" Joey screamed. "I've got to watch Red Sweeny!"

The sound of Joey's piercing voice brought all the heads around. Jim Newton saw the squirming boy twist quickly, breaking the guard's hold on his shoulder.

The loudspeaker roared the announcement, "Red Sweeny, coming out of chute two on Thunder Lady!"

Before the echo died down, the frenzied boy leaped onto the iron rail, dropped into the arena, and dashed in front of the chutes.

"*Hold it!*" the speaker blared. "*Hold the gate!*"

Jim saw that it was too late to hold anything; Red Sweeny had already dropped into the saddle. In one violent motion, Jim sprang from his seat and vaulted over the rail onto the ground. Lunging forward, he clamped a hand on Joey's arm and jerked him aside, just as the chute gate slammed open and the bucking bronc stormed into the arena. The flailing hind hoofs missed Jim's head by a fraction of an inch.

A shocked cry went up as the crowd rose to its feet. Jim held Joey close to the wall as Red Sweeny stuck in his saddle and went on to qualify. Red had had no realization of what was happening; he'd been too busy to see anything but his bronc's ears.

The cheers and applause were deafening as Jim boosted Joey over the rail and climbed up after him. The loudspeaker opened up again: "That was a very courageous action! Let's give that man a big hand!"

After everyone applauded and cheered again, the announcer added a stern warning: "That was a near tragedy—that boy might have been killed. Anyone else who pulls a foolish stunt like that will be dealt with by the authorities. . . . Now—let's go on with the bronc-riding!"

When Jim and Joey were seated, Pete gave Jim a steely look. "Jim," he said, "you mighta been killed, too. Them hoofs didn't miss you by no more'n a hair, you realize that?" Jim nodded. Pete dropped his stern expression, reached across Joey, and stuck out his hand. "Congratulations, boss—that took real guts."

"I'm not so sure of that," Jim said. "It was plain reflex action." He spoke to the trembling boy beside him. "Well, son, how do you feel?"

Before Joey could answer, the guard stormed into the front row, demanding that Jim turn the boy over to him to be ejected. Jim refused, saying that he would be responsible for the boy and would pay for his ticket after the rodeo was over. The guard argued angrily but lost his point and stomped up the steps in a rage.

Joey, still pale and shaking, laid his hand on Jim's arm. "Gee, mister," he said in a small voice, "I don't know how to thank you—I mean for everything."

"Forget it, son," Jim said gently. "Enjoy the rodeo."

Joey was perplexed. "Aren't you gonna give me a bawling out for what I did?"

"Nope, I think you've learned your lesson. Am I right?"

Joey nodded. "Yes, sir. The reason I jumped down there was because I was afraid I'd be thrown out and miss the rodeo. You see, I didn't have any money, so I—I sneaked in."

"*Sneaked in?*" Pete said. "If you ask me, you roared in like an army tank!" He held up his foot. "Here—look what you done to my brand-new boot!"

Joey's face fell. "Golly, did I do that? I'm awful sorry." He leaned down and wiped Pete's boot with his hand.

The old man was ashamed for having lost his temper. "Aw, quit that, an' let's fergit it," he said sheepishly. "I reckon these here boots're too fancy fer an old codger like me, anyways."

Jim chuckled and looked down at Joey. "You haven't told us your name, son."

"Joey Clark."

"Glad to know you, Joey. This is Pete, my ranch foreman. My name's Jim Newton."

"Jim *Newton?*" Joey's eyes were like saucers, and his mouth hung wide open. He turned to Pete. "Is he really Jim Newton?"

"That's his handle, all right."

Joey looked back at Jim in awe. "From the Broken Wheel Ranch?"

"That's right."

Joey could hardly get the next question out. "Then you—you own *Fury?*"

Jim smiled. "Right now it would be more truthful to say that Fury owns *us.*"

"You kin say that agin," Pete added.

In the arena the trick riders and ropers continued to perform, but Joey wasn't concerned with their actions. Without seeming to pause for a breath, he told the two men how he had read the story in the newspaper that morning; how crazy he was about horses; and how he'd even give his right arm to meet Fury face to face.

"No need to go that far," Jim said. "You can meet Fury any time you like."

"You really mean that?" Joey asked in a high voice. "How?"

"Easy. Get your dad to drive you out someday. Will you do that?"

Joey's face fell. "Sure," he said huskily. "I'll ask my—my dad. Thanks, Mr. Newton."

Jim gave Joey a sidewise glance. He sensed that the boy was troubled but decided not to question him at the moment. Hearing a burst of applause, he looked into the arena and saw that the trick riding and roping event was over, and the tramp clown was riding out on his trained burro. The clown cuddled a small, squirming pig under his arm, and when it jumped down and ran squealing across the field, everybody roared with laughter.

The next event was bulldogging, and Joey remembered that Red Sweeny was entered. He stood up and looked toward the chutes, but Red hadn't yet appeared. While he was still craning his neck, Joey heard someone call his name. The stern voice sounded familiar, and when he turned he saw Mr. Taylor. The superintendent was standing in the aisle at the end of the row with the guard, who was leering at Joey in triumph. Mr. Taylor had a determined look on his face.

"Come out of there, Joey!" Mr. Taylor commanded. "I'm taking you home!"

Joey went cold all over. "Oh, no—not yet! *Please!*" he begged.

"Who's that?" Pete asked. "Yer father?"

"Uh—not exactly," Joey said. "He's a friend of mine." For some reason he didn't want his new friends to know that he had no father.

"Come on, Joey!" Mr. Taylor called.

Jim patted Joey's arm. "Sorry, Joey, but if you know that man I guess you'd better go."

"No, Mr. Newton—I don't want to!" There was panic in his voice.

"Down in front!" somebody shouted.

The guard began to push past the people in the row, so Joey looked around for an escape. He was determined not to go back with Mr. Taylor and be

punished that afternoon, even if he had to miss the
rest of the rodeo. He looked down at Jim and gasped,
"Thanks, Mr. Newton—for everything. You, too, Pete."

Turning his back on the oncoming guard, he shoved
past Pete, bringing his heel down hard on the old fellow's boot.

"Dang it!" Pete exploded. "You got the other one!"

Joey rushed in front of the other people in the row,
all of whom stood up hastily to let him get by. He
reached the opposite aisle and raced up the steps to the
exit from the seating section. As he looked across the
heads of the crowd he saw Mr. Taylor climbing the
steps of his own aisle, two at a time, and making angry
gestures. Joey ran down the incline to the alley under
the grandstand and continued out through the main
gate of the Fairgrounds. Glancing back, he saw Mr.
Taylor just emerging from the alley.

Joey glanced left and right, then sprinted straight
ahead to the parking lot, where he knew he could
take refuge among the cars. Once on the lot he found
it easy to lose himself among the many rows of vehicles. A great burst of cheers came from the grandstand, and when it died down he again heard Mr.
Taylor calling his name. From the sound of his voice,
Joey knew his pursuer wasn't too far away. He snaked
in and out among the cars, looking desperately for a
safe place to hide. Suddenly, between a pickup truck
and a fancy convertible, he saw something that gave
him the answer to his problem. It was a station wagon,
with *Broken Wheel Ranch* painted on the side door.
This was luck beyond his wildest dreams. He turned the
handle, and the door opened. He slid in under the steer-
ing wheel, closed the door softly, and climbed over
the back of the seat. On the floor in the rear of the
station wagon was a pile of horse blankets. Lying

flat, he pulled one of the blankets over his body, so that he was completely hidden.

In the quiet darkness he could hear his heart pounding, but although he was exhausted, he felt happy and secure. He lay there listening with his eyes closed. A little later he was sound asleep.

CHAPTER 5

Joey Meets Fury

IT WAS DAYTIME, but Joey was having a nightmare. His dream had started beautifully: a brass band was playing, and when the music stopped a voice on the loudspeaker announced: "And now, ladies and gentlemen, the rodeo champion of the world—*Joey Clark!*"

A tremendous roar went up from ten thousand throats, the gate swung open, and Joey galloped into the arena, mounted on Fury. He swept down the track in front of the grandstand, bowing and waving his ten-gallon hat. As he arrived at the governor's box, the governor signaled for him to stop, and Joey brought Fury to a halt.

It was at this point that the beautiful dream began to turn into a nightmare. When the governor reached out to shake hands, Joey was embarrassed to find that his own right hand was holding a barbecue sandwich. With a sickly grin, he laid the sandwich on his saddle and shook the governor's hand. The governor drew it back quickly, a disgusted expression on his face. Barbecue sauce was running up the governor's arm, and as Joey watched, the sauce turned into white paint. Now it was dripping onto the man's blue suit. The crowd groaned and rose to its feet. Joey exclaimed, "Golly, did I do that? I'm awfully sorry," and leaned across the rail to wipe the paint off with his hand. The governor grabbed Joey's arm and cried, "Caughtcha!" Joey began to struggle, and while he was squirming the man's face changed completely. It became the fat, angry face of the guard. Joey wrenched his hand loose, and the guard put his foot up on the rail. On his foot was a yellow boot with a big ugly gouge in it. The guard jumped down into the arena, and Joey started to run.

As in all nightmares, strange things happened for no logical reason, and Joey was no longer mounted on Fury. Instead he was on foot, racing up and down the rows of cars on the parking lot, desperately trying to find the station wagon with *Broken Wheel Ranch* painted on the door. He heard footsteps running close behind him and Mr. Taylor's voice calling his name, but nowhere could he find the station wagon. The rows of parked vehicles seemed to stretch to the horizon, and Joey was seized with panic as he ran with bursting lungs, searching frantically for the one car that would mean safety and freedom.

Suddenly, the parking lot was filled with laughing, shouting people, all getting into their cars. He heard doors slamming, and the sound of motors starting. One door slammed more loudly than the others, and Joey awoke from his nightmare.

Confused and groggy, he pawed the blanket away from his face and rose up on one elbow. The motor started, and he heard Pete's voice just above his head.

"Okay on this side, Jim."

Joey's mind cleared in an instant and he glanced up. Jim was at the wheel with Pete beside him, so Joey ducked his head back under the blanket and lay still. He felt the station wagon pull out of the row and heard the crunch of wheels turning slowly on gravel. Voices faded in and out as the station wagon passed groups of people.

One deep voice shouted, "Hey, Jim, congrats for rescuing that crazy kid! Just like in the movies!"

"Nothing to it, Ben," Jim called good-naturedly. "They do it every day on TV."

Joey heard Pete's cackling laugh. "See there, Jim? You're a big hero in these parts. Reckon ya'll be gittin' a movie contract any day now."

"One more crack like that and you'll walk back to the ranch," Jim commented drily.

Joey felt the car move onto a smooth roadbed and pick up speed. He knew that if he could just lie there quietly he wouldn't be discovered until they reached the Broken Wheel Ranch. He hoped that Jim and Pete wouldn't be too angry when they found him, but his fear of their wrath faded with the exciting realization that he was actually going to meet Fury. His only worry now was that the dusty, prickly blanket over his face might make him sneeze. After a few minutes of silence, he heard Pete's voice from the front seat.

"You ain't what I'd call extry talkative on this trip, Jim."

"Uh?" Jim grunted, as though his mind were far away.

"I reckanize that thoughtful look in your eye," Pete went on. "Yer mind's on that wild kid Joey, ain't it?"

"Matter of fact, it is."

"Somethin' real screwy about that boy. Him turnin' white as a sheet when that feller come down the aisle sayin' he was takin' him home. Then when I ast Joey if it was his father, he said 'not exac'ly.'" For a minute there was quiet, then Pete continued, "If that feller wasn't his father, then why did he say he was takin' Joey home?"

"I don't know, Pete, but it was obvious that Joey was frightened half out of his wits."

"He shore was. As spooked as a cow that stepped in a nest of rattlers."

Joey heard the crackle of cellophane.

"Want a smoke, Jim?" Pete asked.

"No, thanks."

Joey listened, feeling that it was wrong to eavesdrop, but knowing that if he were to throw the blanket off and speak to them, the men would turn around and drive him straight back to town. Since he'd come this far, he wasn't going to spoil his chance to see Fury.

"Ya know, there was somethin' I liked about that young critter," Pete resumed, "even if he did leave his heel brand on these here new boots of mine."

Jim laughed. "I'm glad you feel that way, Pete, because I liked him, too."

Joey smiled under the blanket and felt goose-bumps all over his body. He'd wanted desperately to have these men like him, and now he'd actually heard them say that they did.

"Wonder if we'll ever see him agin," Pete said.

"I have a hunch we will," Jim answered. "Very soon, too."

Joey had to stifle a giggle with his hand. Very soon is right, he thought.

"He said he'd give his right arm to meet Fury," Jim went on. "So, before too long, he'll show up at the Broken Wheel."

The two men dropped the subject of Joey and talked about the rodeo for the remainder of the trip. Joey was pleased when he heard them remark that Red Sweeny had won a fat purse for bronc-riding. He wished that he had been there to see Red's ride, but at least Red and his stomach would be on good terms with each other, and that satisfied Joey. He hoped he'd see Red again someday. In his book Red was a real champ and a swell fellow.

The sun was just disappearing behind the ridge when Jim Newton drove the station wagon through the gate of the Broken Wheel Ranch. As the car took the small rise toward the corrals, Pete stiffened and shouted, "Holy smokes—look there!"

He was pointing toward Fury's corral. Jim took one look, stopped the car, and leaped out. Inside the corral, Bart was backed against the fence, calling for help. Fury had him cornered. The irate horse was standing on his hind legs, striking out at Bart with his forefeet. His teeth were bared and his ears were laid back. Pete, just a step behind Jim, saw Hank tearing down from the bunkhouse. Meantime, Bart was howling for help.

Jim sprang to the bottom rail of the fence and leaned into the corral. A second later, Pete was up beside him.

"Grab his other arm!" Jim shouted.

Fury was snorting angrily. His tail was erect, and his sharp hoofs were beating the air, only inches from Bart's face. Just as Hank arrived, Jim and Pete gave a tremendous heave and jerked Bart up over the top rail, almost pulling his arms from their sockets. He landed on the ground outside the corral. His face was purple with rage. For a moment he lay there wheezing, too breathless to form the abusive words in his mind.

Jim whirled on Hank. "I thought I told you not to let Bart go inside this corral!"

"You did, boss," Hank said guiltily. "But I was up yonder takin' a snooze, an' I thought Bart was, too."

Pete tried to help Bart to his feet, but the man batted Pete's hand away and stood up, unsteadily. He glared at Fury and shook his fist.

"I'll bust you, by thunder!" he croaked. "Ya hear me, ya black murderer? I'll bust ya if it's the last thing I ever do!"

Jim's face was stormy. "It will be the last thing you ever do if you don't follow orders! I told you to try to gentle him down from a safe distance."

"I did try!" Bart sputtered. "I been tryin' fer the last twenny minutes, but it didn't do no good!"

Jim was scanning the ground inside the corral.

"Ya won't find no club in there!" Bart rasped. "Ya said not to rough him up, an' I wasn't tryin' to." He pointed to a spot near the fence, halfway down the inclosure. "I had that hackamore, see? I was on'y tryin' to slip it on, but he come at me like before. Jist doin' my job, that's all," he added, self-righteously.

Fury pranced along the railing, picked the hackamore up in his teeth, and shook it angrily. The men knew that the rope halter wouldn't last long under that kind of punishment. Bart shuffled away from the others and stood glaring at the horse. His lips kept moving; it was obvious that he was saying something to his four-footed enemy that wouldn't be acceptable in polite company.

As the other three men watched Fury punishing the hackamore, Hank caught sight of something out of the corner of his eye. "Well, fer gosh sakes," he said, "we got us a visitor."

Jim and Pete followed Hank's glance. There was Joey hurrying along the fence toward Fury!

"Joey!" Jim exclaimed in disbelief.

"Danged if it ain't!" Pete said.

Joey's eyes were popping, and his face was one big grin as he stopped outside the fence a few feet from the agitated horse. "Fury!" he murmured, in a voice full of wonder and worship. "*Fury!*"

The stallion stopped worrying the hackamore and stared at the boy. Joey raised one foot to step on the bottom rail, but Jim had sensed this move and was standing over him before Joey's shoe touched the wood. The boy felt himself being yanked off the ground by his shoulders and shaken like a rag.

Jim had reached the limit of his patience. "Dog-gone it!" he exploded. "I'm sick and tired of pulling foolish people out of scrapes! What's the matter with you? Haven't you got any sense at all? First you run in front of a bronc chute, and now you want to get yourself torn apart by a wild horse's teeth! Don't you know that an angry mustang stallion is about the most dangerous animal alive?"

Joey cringed under the violent scolding as though he'd been whipped. Pete felt it necessary to add to Jim's warning with his own bitter comment.

"What in tarnation you got inside your head instead-a brains? One bite with them big teeth an' you'd be a goner!" Pete took off his hat and scratched his head. "An' now that me an' Jim've got all that off our chests, what're you doin' on this ranch, anyways? How'd ya git here?"

Joey pointed toward the station wagon. "I drove out with you," he said, in a small, frightened voice.

Pete scowled. "Whattaya mean, ya drove out with us? Are you plumb loco?"

Joey looked at the ground, guiltily. "I was in the back, under a blanket."

Jim cocked his head in amazement. "Joey, is that the truth?"

Joey nodded.

"Wal, how do ya like that!" Pete said. "A stowaway! Dang it all, Joey, if I was your father an' had a son as wild as you, I'd wallop your hide good!"

"Yes, sir," Joey whispered. "I guess maybe you'd have a right to."

Jim noticed that the boy's eyes were damp at the corners. His anger had subsided by this time, so he knelt down and spoke in a more gentle voice.

"Why did you do it, Joey?"

"I—I wanted to see Fury."

"But I told you, you were welcome to come out and see Fury any time at all. Your father could have driven you out whenever he felt like it."

"Yes, Mr. Newton, I know," Joey said miserably.

"Wal, by this time," Pete said, "yer father must be havin' conniption fits about ya. Now he'll hafta drive all the way out here an' pick ya up. I'll go in an' call him. What's yer phone number?"

Joey thought fast. "Uh—my father hasn't got a phone."

"He ain't? That's funny. Doggone it, Jim," Pete complained, "now one of us has got to drive Joey all the way back inta town." He peered at Jim through his shaggy eyebrows. "An' I bet a new saddle it'll be me."

"That's right," Jim said. "I've got a lot of paperwork to do tonight." He turned to Joey. "All right, son, get back into the station wagon."

"No, wait!" Joey begged. "Please! Can't I watch Fury for a little while?"

Jim considered a moment. "Well, okay—watch him if you want to. But that's all you'll be able to do. He won't let you get near him."

"Maybe he'll feel different about *me*," Joey said. "You see, Mr. Newton, I really love horses a lot."

Pete snorted. "We don't exactly hate horses around here, Joey. An' you seen what Fury jist done to Jim's bronc-buster. If me an' Jim hadn't come along when we did, Bart would-a been a case fer the undertaker."

"I know," Joey argued. "But that man doesn't love Fury—he hates him. I could tell by the way he shook his fist at him—and the mean things he said."

Jim glanced back at Bart and Hank, who were heading for the bunkhouse.

"Joey," Jim said patiently, "what do we have to do

to prove to you that Fury won't let anybody get close to him? Just look at him." He pointed to Fury, who still stood a few yards inside the corral, shaking the hackamore in savage protest.

Joey looked at the angry horse and grinned. "Boy, he sure is mad." He shook his head in admiration. "Mr. Newton, can I just talk to him a minute?"

"Well, certainly, if you want to," Jim agreed. "It's the right thing to do. I was telling Bart just this noon that the only way to gentle a wild horse down is to get him used to the sound of the human voice. But stand right here, Joey, don't go any closer."

"Okay," Joey said eagerly.

Behind Joey's back, Pete caught Jim's eye and pointed to the darkening sky. In pantomime, with his finger, he indicated the station wagon, the gate, the road to town, and the trip back to the ranch. Then he pointed to his stomach to show that he was hungry.

Jim nodded, understandingly. "I'll fix supper," he whispered. "Let's give him a couple of minutes."

Pete threw up his hands, as if to indicate that the whole world was crazy except himself. Spying a pebble that he suddenly seemed to hate, he kicked it viciously.

"Act your age," Jim muttered sternly. "Give the boy a chance."

Unaware of the byplay behind his back, Joey was giving all his attention to Fury. "Fury," he called in a low, loving voice. "Fury—it's me, Joey."

The horse, if he heard, was not impressed. His particular project was to tear the hated rope bridle to bits. He threw his head back and flung the hackamore into the air to get a better hold on it with his coarse, white teeth.

Joey raised his voice a little. "Fury . . ." There was no reaction. "Fury!" he repeated sharply.

Fury jerked his head toward the small figure on the opposite side of the fence. The stallion's large eye-balls stood out whitely in the gathering darkness. The mangled bridle hung limply from his mouth.

Now that Joey had the animal's attention, he spoke without sharpness. "Hi, there, boy . . . hi."

Fury's ears sprang up like a jack-in-the-box. He lowered his head and stared at Joey, his big, round nostrils wide open. Joey extended his right hand, palm upward. The white eyeballs swiveled down to the hand.

"Fury—come here."

The frightened eyes leaped back to Joey's face.

"Come on, boy—take a step. . . . Come on, Fury—don't be scared. . . . Please don't—I love you. . . . Can't you tell?" Joey was begging, entreating—almost crooning.

Slowly—very slowly—Fury stretched his neck toward the imploring boy. His nostrils flared and pulsated, searching for a scent. Nothing broke the stillness but the sound of his rapid sniffing, like a bellows being operated at high speed.

"Come on, boy—I won't hurt you. . . . Come on," said the soothing voice.

Fury looked at the outstretched hand again and took a pace forward. Jim and Pete exchanged surprised glances and looked back at the pleading boy. At that moment, Joey disobeyed orders and took a step toward the fence. Pete extended his arm, anxiously, but Jim held up a restraining hand. A sixth sense told him not to break the spell.

"Good boy, Fury," Joey said. "Now come on—try again." Fury stood still, wary but tempted. "Come on, Fury—come on."

Fury turned his head and looked to the rear, as though checking his avenue of escape if it should be necessary. He looked at Joey again, hesitated a second, then stepped obediently up to the fence. Joey glanced at Jim, silently asking permission. Jim hesitated for two heartbeats, then nodded. With his hand held out, Joey took the two steps which brought him to the fence. The horse stood his ground, his head out over the top rail, the bridle dangling from his mouth. Joey took hold of the sodden rope and gave it a gentle tug. Fury unclenched his teeth and released it, and the boy dropped the hackamore to the ground. The wild stallion trembled visibly but waited courageously for the first touch of a human hand.

Joey placed his palm on Fury's soft upper lip and rubbed it lovingly. The lip quivered, but Fury stood still, making small, friendly sounds in his throat. The two seasoned horsemen watched the miracle, spellbound, hardly daring to believe what they saw. Joey drew a deep, sobbing breath and stood on tiptoes.

"Oh, Fury," he murmured. "Fury—my *friend*."

Fury flung his head back and nickered proudly, then swung around, and danced gaily into the center of the corral.

Pete let out a whoop and grinned from ear to ear. "Wal, I'll be a son of a horsethief!" he shouted.

Jim called Joey's name. When the boy turned around, big tears were running down his cheeks, but his face was radiant with joy.

CHAPTER 6

Jim Meets Mr. Taylor

JOEY FINISHED his second glass of milk and reached across the table for another one of Pete's homemade cookies. Jim Newton glanced out the ranch-house window and saw the far-off ridge standing black against the last faint light of the evening.

"It's getting pretty late," Jim reminded Joey. "Suppose you put some of those cookies in your pocket and eat them while you're driving back to town."

"Good idea," Pete said. He rummaged through a drawer and took out a paper bag. "I'll put some in a sack for ya, Joey, how'd that be?"

Joey frowned. "Okay—only—" He hesitated and looked up at Jim.

"Only what?" Jim asked.

Joey took a bite out of the cookie and swallowed it before answering. "I don't want to go back. I told you that, Mr. Newton. I want to stay here at the ranch."

Jim sighed. "Look, Joey, we've already gone over that subject two or three times. Now, you're an intelligent boy, and you should understand that you've *got* to go home—right away. By this time your parents must be crazy with worry."

"No, they're not," Joey said truthfully. "Honest."

Jim looked at Pete, shook his head, and walked to the fireplace. As he gazed down at the crackling logs, he wondered how he was going to cope with the problem. He knew exactly how to handle an obstinate colt or a stubborn mule, but this boy baffled him completely. Joey was acting precisely like an obstinate colt, yet he was a thinking human being. Jim had an unaccustomed feeling of helplessness.

When Joey had persuaded Fury to allow himself to be touched—a miraculous feat that had been impossible even for experienced horsemen—Jim had felt the pride of a father in an extraordinary achievement of his son. He had walked with Joey into the ranch-house, his arm around the boy's shoulders. Both he and Pete had smothered Joey with praise and had gone back over the incredible experience, step by step. Pete said that he had never seen anything to equal Joey's exploit in all his years as a cowpoke and rancher. While getting the cookies and milk, Pete had suddenly felt a strong affection for this mysterious boy, and his heart had been filled with unusual warmth.

Joey himself had never known such happiness. Within the past few hours his life had taken a golden turn, for his dream had sharpened into a reality. He had actually met the tall, bronzed man who worked with horses—and had pleased him. As though that were not enough, he had also met and pacified the famous black mustang. As he finished the cookie, Joey felt confident that the remainder of his dream would come true, also. He would have a horse of his own to train, groom, and ride—and his name would be Fury.

In Joey's state of elation it had never occurred to him that Jim would send him back to his old life. But when Jim insisted, a sudden chill gripped Joey, and he grew stubborn. The more Jim and Pete urged him to get ready for the return drive, the more firmly Joey stood on his resolve never to return to the Home.

Jim came back from the fireplace and sat down

beside Joey at the table. "Joey," he said firmly, "you must start back right away. What's your address in town?"

Joey paused before giving his answer. "I'm sorry, Mr. Newton, but I won't tell you."

Jim looked at Pete for help, and the old man came over and sat down at the opposite side of the table. "Look," he snapped, "quit actin' like a mule. I gotta drive you all the way in, then drive myself back agin, so cut horsin' around and tell us where you belong."

"Okay," Joey said quietly, "I'll tell you." The anxious men leaned forward eagerly. "I belong right here at the Broken Wheel Ranch."

Pete made an exasperated sound and jumped up to get his pipe. Jim gave the table a hard slap and spoke in a stern voice.

"If you were *my* son," he began, "I'd—" he stopped and concluded lamely—"I don't know what I'd do."

Joey looked at Jim with big, wide eyes. "If I *were* your son, Mr. Newton," he said earnestly, "I'd do whatever you told me to."

Jim flushed and felt vaguely pleased, for a reason he didn't understand. "That's a nice compliment, Joey," he said with a smile, "but you're not my son. And as I was saying, your parents must be worried." He laid his hand on Joey's arm. "Pete and I are very happy to have you here, and you may come out again, any time you want to. But when a boy has a home, he can't just walk away from it." Jim stood up. "So come on, Joey, I'll walk you out to the station wagon."

Joey sat still. "I'm not going," he said.

Pete blew out a cloud of smoke and spoke to Jim. "Want me to pick him up like a sack o' flour an' carry him out?"

Jim shrugged. "I guess you'll have to."

The old foreman set his pipe down carefully in the

ashtray and took Joey's arm. "Okay, boy, let's git goin'."

Joey pulled his arm away and jumped up. His eyes were flashing. "You don't have to carry me out!" he cried. "I'll walk out by myself!"

"Now yer talkin' sense," Pete said.

"But when we get to town," Joey added defiantly, "I won't tell you where I live!" He stood glaring at the two men, breathing heavily.

The men glared back, wondering what to do next. Finally, Pete took hold of Jim's shirt sleeve and drew him into a corner.

"I never seen the like of that young critter," Pete whispered. "What the heck do we do now?"

"I don't know—I've got to think."

Pete pointed to the bookshelf. "You got a whole mess o' books there. Ain't there one that tells how to handle boys?"

Jim shook his head. "Not that I know of."

"Wal, we shore got to do somethin' pretty quick. I'm gittin' so hungry, my stummick thinks my throat's cut."

Jim looked across the room and considered Joey for a few seconds. Then he made a decision. "Joey, I'm going to phone the sheriff."

Joey's face fell. "The *sheriff?* What for?"

"Because by this time your family must have reported you missing."

Jim started for the telephone, but Joey ran to it and held it down.

"No, Mr. Newton! Don't call the sheriff, *please!*"

Jim folded his arms. "All right, I won't call him—yet. But I'll give you just two minutes to tell us where you live." He paused. "Two minutes to talk, Joey, or the call goes in."

Joey bit his lower lip and thought it over. The fact

that he had no parents and lived in an institution was the very last thing he wanted these men to know. What could he tell them? His thoughts were jumbled, and he felt cornered.

Jim waited for the information. When it didn't come, he said, "Joey, this afternoon you ran away from that man at the rodeo. You told us he wasn't your father. Was that the truth?"

"Yes, sir," Joey murmured.

"Then who in tarnation *was* he?" Pete asked.

Joey hesitated. "Mr. Taylor."

"That ain't no answer! Who's Mr. Taylor? How come you was so all-fired scared of him?"

Joey looked at the floor. "Please don't make me tell you," he begged.

At that moment the probable truth of the situation leaped into Jim's mind, and he was angry with himself for not having realized it before. He also felt a great wave of compassion for this boy who stood before him in such torment, understandably, but needlessly, fearing to have his secret known. Jim faced Joey and took him by the shoulders.

"Son," Jim said gently, "do you believe that Pete and I are your friends?"

Joey looked up and nodded. He was too close to tears to speak.

"Okay, then," Jim went on. "As your friends we'll always play straight with you. Now suppose you play straight with us." He knelt down to Joey's eye-level. "You say that Mr. Taylor is not your father, and we believe you. All right so far?"

"Yes, sir."

"Joey," Jim said with great sympathy, "at last I think I know why you're acting this way." He drew a deep breath. "I believe that you haven't a father." Jim felt the frail shoulders slump beneath his hands. "Am I right?"

"Yes, sir," the boy said, in a voice so low and pain-racked that the words were hardly audible. The tears fell freely now—there was no way of holding them back.

Pete saw the agony in Joey's face, then turned his head away and reached for his bandanna. He didn't want Jim to notice that his own eyes were acting strangely. After dabbing at them and blowing his nose furiously, he glanced back and saw that Jim was sitting on the sofa with his arms around the sobbing boy.

At last Joey's story had been told. He had given Jim and Pete all the facts about his life at the Home and had described his dreams of the life that he really wanted. The men had listened sympathetically and had asked understanding questions. After it was over, Joey felt that a great weight had been lifted from his mind and agreed with Jim that Mr. Taylor should be telephoned at once.

At the other end of the line, Mr. Taylor was tremendously relieved to learn that Joey was safe and in good hands. He insisted, of course, that the runaway be returned to the institution as soon as possible, and Jim promised to deliver Joey within a few hours. The worried superintendent said that he had reported the missing boy to the police and that he would notify police headquarters immediately to have the search called off.

Within a half hour after Jim had hung up, Pete had a warm supper on the table, and Joey cleaned his plate without any difficulty. Delighted by the comfortable atmosphere of the ranchhouse and the affection shown him by his new friends, Joey no longer dreaded his return to the Children's Home. He knew that these strong, kindly men liked him and respected him, and deep down in his heart a faint hope was stirring. Several times during his years at the institution he had said good-by to boys who had gone happily away to live with new parents. Although he didn't understand the legal details of these moves, he realized that adoption was possible. Wisely, however, Joey decided not to mention the subject during the meal. He knew that he would return to visit the Broken Wheel Ranch and felt that in due time the hope that was in his heart might turn into a reality.

While they were eating, Joey asked scores of eager questions about Fury, other horses, and ranch life in general. His knowledge wasn't extensive, but his questions were intelligent, and the two ranch men answered them with pleasure and enthusiasm. They were both delighted by Joey's alertness and genuine interest in their work. His very presence at their usually quiet table seemed to add youthful exuberance and excitement that they had been missing without realizing it.

During the animated conversation, a certain agreeable possibility suggested itself to Jim. When the meal ended he gave Joey a picture book about horses to examine, and joined Pete in the kitchen. The two men discussed Jim's idea for ten or fifteen minutes, then Jim returned to Joey and told him that it was time to leave for town.

"Pete will stay here, and I'll drive you in," Jim said. "I had some work to do tonight, but it can wait. Besides, I'd like to meet this Mr. Taylor of yours."

Joey gave a wry smile. "Boy, I bet he'll have it in for me for going AWOL."

"Well, you must admit you deserve some punishment," Jim said solemnly. "But cheer up," he grinned. "Maybe it'll only be KP."

Pete came in at the end of Jim's statement. "What-taya mean, *only* KP?" he asked, with a twinkle. "That's what I been doin' on this here ranch for the last ten years, an' all I got to show fer it is dishpan hands."

"Cut it out, Pete, you're breaking my heart," Jim said. "Three square meals a day and all the fresh air you can breathe, and yet you're griping."

Pete grimaced at Jim and put his hand out for Joey to shake. "So long, Joey, I'll be seein' ya," the old man said with a wink.

Joey winked back and grinned. "I sure hope so, Pete."

Jim draped his arm around Joey's shoulders and opened the door. "Okay," he said. "Off we go into the wild blue yonder."

As the headlights of the station wagon cut across Fury's corral, Fury jerked his head up and nickered.

"G'by, Fury!" Joey shouted. "I'll be seeing *you,* too."

Before the car reached the main road to town, the exhausted boy dropped off to sleep, with his head resting on Jim's right arm.

At the Children's Home, Jim was pleased to dis-cover that Mr. Taylor wasn't anything like the angry demon he had expected him to be. On the contrary, the man was pleasant and courteous, and grateful to Jim for having taken such good care of his missing charge. Aware of the fact that Joey was almost asleep on his feet, Mr. Taylor said, "I'm glad to have you back, Joey," and sent him off to bed. Joey mumbled a sleepy thank you and good night to Jim and toiled slowly up the stairs.

When Joey had reached the top step safely, Mr.

Taylor invited Jim into his study for coffee and a talk. After they were settled in deep leather chairs, the superintendent said, "Well, Mr. Newton, what do you think of my problem child?"

"I think he's a great boy, Mr. Taylor."

The man smiled. "So do I." He looked at Jim, quizzically. "But how did you find that out in such a short time?"

Jim settled back and began to talk. He told of his and Pete's great fondness for Joey and described everything that the boy had done and said while at the Broken Wheel Ranch. The superintendent didn't seem to be at all surprised by any of the facts.

"Well, Mr. Taylor," Jim concluded, "nothing that I told you seemed to astonish you—not even my description of Joey's meeting with Fury."

The superintendent shook his head. "Why should I be astonished by that? Fury is wild and untamed—but then, so is Joey. Perhaps it takes a wild one to tame a wild one."

"Maybe so," Jim said. "But to tame a wild horse it also takes love, understanding, and intelligence. Joey has all of those qualities." Jim took a sip of coffee and looked up. "What does it take to tame a wild boy?"

Mr. Taylor sighed. "It takes something that a boy can't possibly get in an institution—the affectionate, personal, continuous guidance of parents. According to the records, Joey's mother is dead, and his father abandoned him when the boy was an infant. That's my heartbreaking problem here, Mr. Newton. Every single one of my boys needs the blessings of home life and at least one parent."

Jim set his cup down and leaned forward. "That's what I'd like to talk to you about, Mr. Taylor."

The superintendent beamed. "I know. While you

were telling me about Joey, I recognized that incipient parental gleam in your eye."

"Would it be possible?" Jim asked eagerly.

"It might be—after certain investigations and legal formalities."

Jim grinned and leaped to his feet. "What do I do first?"

"Talk to your lawyer. He'll arrange a court hearing."

"That's easy," Jim said. "Hand me that phone."

Upstairs, in his white enamel bed, Joey was sleeping soundly. It was the bed that he had done all his dreaming in—and it must have been a lucky one.

At the court hearing a week later, Judge Morris approved the adoption and issued a temporary order. The temporary decree meant that at some time in the future the court would consider an application to make the adoption final. During the trial period, Joey would be permitted to live with his adopting parent.

Immediately after Judge Morris handed down his decision, Joey packed his things and drove with Jim Newton to his new home on the Broken Wheel Ranch.

CHAPTER 7

The One-Boy Horse

FOR THE FIRST TIME since he could remember, Joey was completely happy. Everything about his new life at the Broken Wheel pleased him: the men, the ranch, and the large, sprawling house. Jim had given him a bedroom to himself, and to his delight the boy discovered that the west window faced Fury's corral.

A day or two after Joey had settled down in his new home, Jim enrolled him in the valley school, which was maintained for the children of the ranchers. Joey's teacher, Miss Miller, was a pleasant, pretty young woman who was both liked and respected by her students. On Joey's first morning at the school, the teacher introduced him to his classmates.

"Boys and girls," Miss Miller announced, "I'd like you to welcome a newcomer to our school: Joey Newton—Jim Newton's son."

The children applauded, and Joey flushed with pride. Never before had he heard himself referred to as anybody's "son," but the three words together: *"Jim Newton's* son," sounded like the grandest title on earth.

During lunch hour Joey's classmates swarmed around him, firing questions about Fury. Having been raised with horses, the children were intensely curious to hear about the now-famous wild stallion. News traveled quickly in the valley, and the story of Joey's first meeting with Fury had received wide circulation among the ranchers and their families. Joey told his enthralled listeners every fact he could remember about Fury, and when he had finished, the children were more anxious than ever to see the great horse with their own eyes. Joey graciously invited them to ride into the Broken Wheel whenever they wanted to and added, with some pride, that he would be happy to give them a personal introduction.

Many of Joey's classmates rode to school on saddle horses of their own. During school hours the animals were tethered in a shady grove behind the building. Joey had never sat astride a horse in his life but was impatient to learn to ride. When classes ended the first day, he walked back to the grove with Peewee Jenkins, a friendly boy who had sat behind him in the classroom. Peewee was several years younger than Joey, and his real name was Rodney; but everyone called him Peewee, because he was the shortest boy in school.

Peewee owned a horse named Pokey, a chestnut mare with white stockings. While Joey was waiting for Hank to pick him up in the station wagon, Peewee gave him a boost into Pokey's saddle and led the horse slowly around the grove. Even though Peewee held onto the bridle, Joey felt that at last he was a horseman and knew that he would always be fond of Peewee for having given him his first ride.

Having been transplanted suddenly from the city to a ranch, Joey discovered that he would have to make a thorough readjustment of his life and habits. He learned quickly that as a member of a small family that worked a horse ranch he would have certain duties to perform. As yet he knew nothing about the care of horses, so his first assignments were menial ones, such as sweeping the porch, keeping his room tidy, and helping Pete in what the old fellow called "manicurin' the goldern dishes."

Joey had no strict supervision at the ranch, but he performed his chores willingly. He actually enjoyed working with Pete in the kitchen, because the old foreman delighted him constantly with exciting stories about his earlier life as a cowpoke. Interspersed among Pete's tales of roundups, rodeos, and bronc-busting were solid practical facts about that noble breed of animal, the horse. The horses Pete liked best were the wild ones, which he said were now growing fewer on the western ranges. He spoke wistfully of the countless wild horses that he had known throughout his life: the roans, the sorrels, the bays, the two-toned pintos and the clown-painted appaloosas. As Joey "manicured the goldern dishes" with Pete, he listened with fascination, absorbing and remembering every fact that he was told.

From the beginning, Joey called his new father "Jim," which suited both of them. As the days wore on, their affection for each other grew greater and stronger, until finally they seldom remembered that they were not actually father and son. In the mornings, late afternoons, and weekends, Joey stayed close to Jim, observing and learning the practical operation of the ranch. Under Jim's instruction he learned the fine points of stabling, feeding, and grooming, as well as the accepted methods of pitching hay and cleaning stalls.

On the first Saturday that they spent together, Jim led a gelding named Cactus from the stable and gave the boy his first lesson in saddling and riding. Joey was an excellent pupil and showed signs of becoming one of those natural riders who are "born to the saddle." Within a few weeks he began to ride Cactus back and forth to school, and felt that at last he really belonged among the native children of the valley.

As Joey moved about the ranch, learning and doing, he was constantly and thrillingly aware of his nearness to Fury. Early each morning and at every free moment during the day, he hurried to the corral and stood close to the fence, talking to the stallion in soft, loving tones. At first, the possibility that Joey might be injured by the untamed animal caused Jim a certain amount of anxiety, but he dismissed his fears when it became apparent that Fury always seemed delighted by Joey's presence. The only rule laid down was that Joey was never to set foot inside the corral until Fury had been completely tamed and broken.

Fury actually seemed to look forward to the frequent visits from his small, human friend. Whenever he saw Joey approaching, he neighed happily and ran quickly to the fence to meet him. Within a short time, Fury allowed Joey to touch every part of his head, and was particularly fond of having his ears scratched.

After a few weeks, Fury permitted Jim, also, to touch his head, but refused to come anywhere near Pete or Hank. Bart simply ignored the horse and made no attempt to approach him. The sullen broncbuster still bore a grudge against Fury for having attacked him that evening when Joey first arrived at the ranch. Bart had not warmed up to Joey, either. He gruffly acknowledged the boy's greeting whenever they met on the ranch but never went out of his way to be friendly or helpful. Secretly, he was vexed by the fact that Joey had been able to overcome Fury's fear of humans, while his own overtures had been violently refused. Joey was naturally aware of Bart's resentment of both Fury and himself and felt uncomfortable in the man's presence. On several occasions he had seen Bart watching him from the neighboring corral with a contemptuous expression on his face. Joey knew that Jim kept Bart on the payroll because he was a good horse wrangler, but the boy wished now and then that Bart would get an itching foot and move on to some other ranch.

Jim and Pete were immensely pleased with Joey's quick adaptation to ranch life. One evening at sunset, the two men were seated on the porch, relaxing and discussing ranch problems. As they talked they could see Joey at the corral, fondling Fury's head. At one point in the conversation, Pete nodded toward Joey and chuckled.

"Jest lookit that boy, Jim. Ain't ya kinda proud of him?"

" 'Proud' isn't the word," Jim answered. "I'm overwhelmed. Joey's the greatest thing that ever happened to me."

"To me, too." The old man looked sideways at his youthful boss. "Jim, do ya ever stop to think what me an' you woulda missed if Joey hadn't went an' stowed away in the station wagon that afternoon?"

Jim frowned. "Sure, I think of it often, and whenever I do I get cold chills." He paused, then added, " You know, Pete, I pity a man who doesn't have a son. Having Joey here every day—teaching him the things I know—makes me realize how empty my life was before he came."

"No emptier'n mine was." Pete heaved a sigh. "I shore wisht I was yore age, Jim. Yore gonna live t'see that boy grow up, an' mebbe take over this ranch someday." He closed his eyes and smiled. "An', by thunder, that'd be somethin' worth seein'!"

Suddenly, Jim sprang to his feet. "*Joey!*" he exclaimed.

Pete's eyes popped open. "Huh?"

Jim pointed toward the corral. Joey had climbed

up on the bottom rail of the fence. His arms were wound tightly around Fury's neck. The men heard Joey's shrill, excited voice:

"Jim—Pete! *Look!*"

Jim leaped over the railing of the porch. As he ran, he heard Joey cry out again:

"Look, Jim! Look what Fury's letting me do!"

Jim slowed down and walked the remainder of the distance, so as not to startle the horse. As he reached Joey's side, the boy looked toward him. Jim saw ecstasy in his face.

"He's never let me do this before!" Joey cried excitedly. "Never once!"

"I know," Jim said, in pleased amazement.

Joey planted a kiss on the top of Fury's broad, black head and jumped down from the rail. There were tears of happiness in his eyes.

"You know something, Jim," Joey said earnestly. "I think Fury's ready for a bridle."

"So do I," Jim agreed. "Wait here—I'll go get one."

As Jim turned and hastened toward the barn, his own eyes were glistening. "Yes, sir-ee," he said aloud. "I sure do pity a man who doesn't have a son."

In June, after school had ended, Joey had many hours each day to devote to Fury's training. As the month wore on, the stallion learned to trust all humans, with the exception of Bart, and allowed everyone but Bart to enter his corral. The day finally arrived when Jim, Joey, and Pete passed through the gate and gingerly placed a saddle upon the horse's back. It was a ticklish job, and at first Fury trembled with anxiety. He soon calmed down, however, and allowed the girth to be tightened beneath his belly. Fury was remarkably intelligent, and now that his fear was gone he seemed anxious to co-operate.

The next step was to accustom the horse to the weight of a man on his back. Jim placed his foot in the stirrup but got no further. Fury kept sidling away, giving Jim no chance to throw his right leg over the saddle. Pete's attempt to mount also ended in failure. The old fellow was chagrined.

"Gosh hang it," he exploded, "how in tarnation can a man climb aboard if the danged horse won't stand still?"

"Let me try," Joey said eagerly. "I'm not as heavy as a man, so maybe Fury won't mind."

Both Jim and Pete were doubtful about allowing Joey to take the risk.

"Please let me," Joey pleaded. "You can hold my arm and if Fury bucks you can yank me right off."

Jim thought it over and finally consented. Pete gave Joey a boost, and the boy thrust his left foot in the stirrup. Fury craned his neck around, saw that his would-be rider was Joey, and stood still.

"Easy, boy—easy," Joey said. With an extra boost from Pete, he threw his right leg up and landed squarely in the saddle. His foot found the stirrup on the opposite side. "Okay, Jim," he said confidently, "let go of my arm."

Jim relinquished his hold, and Joey looked down, grinning in triumph.

"Congratulations, Joey," Jim said proudly. "It looks to me as though Fury's your horse from now on."

"Did you hear that, Fury?" Joey cried gleefully. "Did you hear what Jim said?"

Fury threw his head up and gave a loud neigh.

In the adjoining corral, Bart, who had been watching the activity, turned away in disgust. He had been hoping to see this green kid bucked sky-high, and Joey's victory made his blood boil. If Bart had disliked Fury before this episode, he now hated him with a passion.

For Joey, every day was a glorious adventure. Early each morning he saddled Fury and rode him around the corral. Within a few weeks he was taking daily canters through the meadow, with Jim and Pete riding beside him on their own mounts. By the middle of July, Fury had become so completely trustworthy that Joey was permitted to ride without an escort whenever he pleased. Joey was the horse's only rider, however; Fury never permitted any other person to mount him.

The news about the one-man stallion, or, to be more exact, the one-*boy* stallion, swept the valley. Almost every day, one or more of Joey's classmates rode into the Broken Wheel to visit Joey and Fury and enjoy the thrill and honor of riding beside them. Sometimes the boys and girls were accompanied by their parents who, as ranchers, shared their children's curiosity about Fury.

On the last Saturday morning of July, Charlie Stevens drove his horse van into the ranch to pick up some new stock and, incidentally, to examine Fury with a professional eye. Stevens had not been back to the Broken Wheel since that day in spring, when he had stayed for lunch and had teased Pete about the mustang stallion being a ghost in Pete's imagination. Having approved and paid for his horses, Stevens loaded them into his van, then asked Joey to let him see Fury in action. Never needing to be coaxed into displaying his beloved horse, Joey saddled Fury and rode him proudly back and forth in front of the barn. Stevens stood with Jim and Pete, watching Fury's every move with undisguised admiration.

"By George!" he boomed in his deep voice. "That's

a magnificent piece of horseflesh!" He removed his wide-brimmed Stetson and turned to Pete. "I take my hat off to you, Pete. I remember suggesting to you that this stallion was only a ghost."

"Heh-heh," Pete cackled. "Some ghost." He thrust his chin forward. "I told ya he was a great horse, didn't I?"

"You sure did," the visitor grinned. "But I wasn't convinced until this minute." Fury thundered past the group again, and Stevens waved his arms. "Hold up, Joey," he shouted. "Let me have a close look at that horse."

Joey swung Fury around and cantered back to the men. Stevens stepped forward and gave the stallion a thorough going over with his expert hands. Joey and the others could tell by the man's delighted exclamations that Fury pleased him immensely.

"Congratulations, son," said Mr. Stevens, when the examination was over. "You've done a great job with a great horse."

"Thank you, sir," Joey said, dismounting.

Stevens turned to Jim with a businesslike air. "All right, Jim, let's talk terms. How much do you want for him?"

Joey uttered a sharp cry of dismay and peered at Jim's face. Jim gave the boy a reassuring pat on the shoulder.

"If you're speaking about Fury," Jim said, "he isn't for sale."

Joey sighed with relief and looked at Stevens. The man had an expression of annoyance on his face.

"What do you mean, he isn't for sale?" he asked belligerently. "You're in business to sell horses, aren't you?"

"You know I am, Charlie," Jim answered. "But I meant what I said—Fury isn't for sale."

Stevens whirled around to Pete. "What's got into this boss of yours? You been feeding him loco weed?"

"Nope," Pete said drily. "Jim eats what I eat—an' I ain't crazy yet."

Stevens paused, considering his next move. Finally his face broke into a grin. "Oh, I get it now," he said knowingly. "You've got a great horse here, and you know I've got plenty of money. You're just playing hard-to-get to make me boost my offer." He jabbed Jim in the ribs with his elbow. "Right?"

"No, Charlie, you're dead wrong," Jim said calmly. "You've been buying horses from me long enough to know that I don't do business that way. I'd never take advantage of a man simply because he was well-off." He looked Stevens straight in the eye. "Fury just isn't for sale, and that's that."

"Humph!" Stevens grunted. He lighted a cigar and peered shrewdly through the smoke. "Jim," he continued, gesturing toward the ranchhouse, "I happen to know you've got a pretty hefty mortgage on that house. What I'd pay you for Fury would take a big load off your mind and put it in your bank account."

Jim glanced toward the house. There was a thoughtful expression on his face and Joey noticed it. With fear in his heart, the miserable boy turned to Fury and placed his cheek against the soft muzzle.

"Come on, Jim," Stevens prodded. "You could use the money and you know it. What do you say?"

Joey held his breath, waiting for Jim's answer. Jim looked at Joey and his eyes softened. "Fury isn't my property," he said. "He belongs to Joey."

Joey turned and spoke in a low, quavering voice. "Jim—if you really need money—it's okay with me if you—" his voice broke and trailed off into a sob— "want to sell Fury."

Jim put his arms around the boy's shoulders. "Thank

you, son," he whispered softly, "but I don't need money that badly." He turned to Stevens and spoke almost harshly. "Sorry, Charlie—no deal."

Stevens threw his cigar to the gravel and ground it under his heel. As a man of wealth, he had been accustomed to getting everything he wanted, and he was eager to possess this magnificent stallion. Knowing Jim, however, he realized that he was defeated; that Jim's decision was final.

"Okay," Stevens said, "there's no arguing with a fool. But let me tell you one thing," he added, pointing to Fury. "You won't be able to control that animal for any length of time. He started out as a wild, vicious beast—a killer—and, mark my words, someday he'll revert to type. That's the day you'll remember my offer and hate yourself for turning it down!"

The rancher turned on his heel, climbed into his van, and drove away at a reckless speed.

Pete took off his dusty hat and slapped his thigh with it. "That Stevens," he muttered. "*He's* the one that's been eatin' loco weed."

Joey spoke in a small, frightened voice. "Jim—it isn't true what Mr. Stevens said—is it? Fury won't go back to being wild again—will he?"

"Of course he won't," Jim said, giving Joey a playful jab. "Now, suppose you unsaddle this 'vicious killer' of yours and wash up for lunch."

CHAPTER 8

Raids on the Ranches

NOW THAT Fury had been safely broken to the saddle, Joey was eager to learn other skills required of ranch workers, and found Hank to be an excellent and willing teacher. The good-natured, easygoing bronc-buster had developed a fondness for the boy, and never tired of answering his questions or demonstrating the tricks and mechanical operations of his trade.

The technique of roping fascinated Joey, and Hank spent hours of his own free time showing Joey how to run out a loop and pick up stationary objects. Joey found roping to be a great deal more difficult than it looked in the movies or on TV, and despaired of ever learning to pick up a moving target, such as a running bronc. Hank assured him that skill with a rope requires patience, practice, and a knowledge of the essentials. The essentials, he said, were a sense of timing and rhythm, and the ability to estimate distances instantly.

Late one afternoon, when Jim, Pete, and Bart were in the hills rounding up some new stock, Joey had an opportunity to watch Hank break a wild pony. The boy sat on the top rail of the cedar-pole corral and listened to Hank's preliminary explanation.

"Ya almost always start when a pony's a three-year-old," Hank began. "An' the idea is ta first get a hackamore on him."

84

"A hackamore," Joey said. "That's what Bart tried to put on Fury the day I first came out here."

"That's right." Hank's eyes twinkled. "Pore old Bart —he ain't been the same since."

Joey frowned. He didn't want to talk about Bart; he preferred to stay on more pleasant subjects. When he had seen Bart ride out with the others, he had felt relieved. He changed the subject by asking a question. "Hank, why do you use a hackamore instead of a bridle?"

" 'Cause a hackamore don't have a steel bit like a bridle," Hank explained. "Ya see, a young bronc don't know enough not to fight a steel bit, an' he might git his mouth tore up. Savvy?"

Joey nodded. Hank hitched up his jeans and adjusted his loop.

"Okay," he grinned, "here goes nothin'."

The bronc-peeler jumped down into the corral, lifted his saddle from the rail, and walked toward the group of four ponies. The suspicious animals edged away and huddled together, sniffing the air. Hank had chosen a small gray as his first customer. When he had gauged the distance properly he let fly with his rope, and the loop settled around the pony's neck. The startled gray gave a cry and fell back, pulling the rope taut. Hank dug his heels into the ground, and the tug of war began. The lunging animal dragged the man a short distance, and Joey saw Hank's boot heels digging ridges into the dirt like a plowshare. When the pony reached the fence on the far side, it stopped short, and Hank went up the rope, hand over hand. Before the frenzied animal had found time to think of its next move, Hank slipped the hackamore over its head, and the first part of the job was completed.

Perched in his high seat on the top rail, Joey applauded and cheered. His excitement grew even more intense as Hank slapped the saddle on the pony's back and forked him for a wild ride. The whooping wrangler stayed in the saddle just long enough to give the pony its first lesson, then leaped down and rejoined Joey at the fence. Hank's chest was heaving, and he was covered with sweat, but he was chuckling, like a man who was satisfied with a job well done.

"Boy, Hank, that was wonderful!" Joey exclaimed.

"Shucks," Hank said modestly, "that critter was kinda easy, compared ta some. Later on I'll show ya how to handle a real mean one."

Joey was incredulous. "You mean sometimes you have even more trouble than *that?*"

"I shore do," Hank panted. "Sometimes one-a them young broncs gits real uppity. That's when I really hafta go to work."

"What do you do then?" Joey asked. "How do you handle one that's real uppity?"

Hank mopped his dripping face with his sleeve. "Wal, Joey, when that happens, a man finds he could shore use a third arm. When a bronc gits rambunctious, ya have a whole lotta things to do at one an' the same time. With one hand ya latch onto his ear an' hold tight. Meantime, ya gotta keep dancin', so's ya don't git kicked or stepped on. Then with the other hand, ya gotta heave the saddle onto his back." Hank shook his head. "That kinda critter shore keeps a man busy."

"Boy, I'll say!" Joey agreed.

"A-course," Hank went on, "sometimes ya can't even git close enough ta grab a-hold of his ear. A sassy horse like that is purty hard ta handle."

"Then how do you break him?" Joey asked eagerly.

"Wal, in tough cases like that ya gotta throw him by ropin' his front legs. Then, while he's layin' on the ground, ya saddle him and stand over him, with one leg on each side. Then ya ease the rope off his legs an' he stands up, takin' ya right up with him in the saddle."

"Gosh, I'd sure like to see that," Joey said. "But after he stands up, what then?"

Hank grimaced. "That's when the lightnin' strikes. A bronc that's been handled like that is red-eyed mad, an' he lets ya know it. When yore goin' down, he's comin' up, an' after a ride like that, a man usually hasta eat his supper off the mantelpiece."

Joey laughed. "Before I try to be a bronc-buster, I think I'd better learn to be an expert roper, don't you?"

"Yeah, Joey," Hank agreed. "I kinda think that would be smarter."

The bronc-peeler climbed out of the corral and began to reel his rope in. When Joey had the loop ready to make a practice throw at the fence post, his attention was distracted by Fury, who had whinnied piercingly in the adjoining corral. The cry sounded weird and urgent.

"What's the trouble with yer pal?" Hank asked.

"I don't know," Joey said, looking across at the stallion. Fury was standing rigid at the western edge of the inclosure. With ears angled forward and tail standing straight out, he was staring intently toward the hills in the distance.

"Fury!" Joey called. "What is it?"

Fury darted a glance at Joey, then turned his head back toward the west.

"Looks like he hears somethin' out there," Hank muttered.

"It sure does. I wonder what it could be." Joey handed the rope to Hank and ran to Fury's corral. "Fury—what is it?" he cried.

Fury paid scant attention to his young master. For

the remainder of the afternoon he stood attentively at the fence, looking out toward the west, making strange, agitated sounds in his throat.

Late that night, when the men returned from the range with a string of new mustangs, Joey was sound asleep in bed. Jim and Pete were dog-tired after their day of riding and turned in as soon as the stock had been corralled and watered.

For several hours after the last light had gone out in the ranchhouse, Fury pranced nervously back and forth along the west fence of his inclosure. Every few minutes he halted to throw back his head and sniff the air. Finally, when an urge within him became too great to resist, he made one swift circuit of the corral, seeking an opening. Finding none, he swung out to the center of the square, turned, and shot forward with increasing speed. Gauging his distance perfectly, he sprang from the ground and cleared the topmost rail of the fence with several inches to spare. A moment later, with the soft grass of the meadow beneath his pounding hoofs, Fury was racing westward through the darkness.

Jim Newton rose early the following morning to check the condition of his new mustangs. As he came down the steps of the porch, he was astonished to see Fury standing quietly outside the gate of his corral. The stallion seemed weary and spent, and his coat and legs were caked with mud. Jim quickly slipped a rope around Fury's neck and led him back inside the inclosure. When Pete appeared at the fence a few minutes later, Jim was busily picking burrs from the long, black mane.

"What in tarnation're you doin'?" Pete called.

Jim held up a hand for silence. "Not so loud. Come here and look."

Pete climbed over the fence and gave a low whistle. "This horse is dead beat," he said. "What happened?"

Jim frowned. "Fury jumped his corral during the night. I found him standing outside the gate."

Pete darted a glance at the ranchhouse. "Does Joey know?"

"I don't think so. He's probably still asleep."

The foreman circled Fury, examining his grimy coat. "He shore went off on a long trip somewheres." He clucked his tongue. "That's real bad news."

Jim nodded. "Let's hope he doesn't make a habit of it."

"Ya gonna tell Joey?" Pete asked.

"Not unless Fury does it again. No need to worry him."

The foreman picked a burr from the tangled mane. "This here critter shore is a mess. If ya don't want Joey to know, it looks like we better git busy and shine him up."

After a half hour of strenuous labor, the two men had Fury's coat cleaned and his mane combed out. Just as they had returned the currying tools to the barn, the telephone jangled, just inside the door. Jim lifted the receiver.

"Broken Wheel Ranch—Jim Newton."

At that moment, Pete heard Joey calling from the porch and went outside to see what he wanted.

Joey, wearing pajamas, came running along the gravel. "Hi, Pete," the boy said, in a voice full of morning energy. "Where's Jim?"

"In the barn, answerin' the phone." Pete took Joey by the arm. "Let's go back inside. You put yer clothes on an' I'll fix breakfast."

A short while later, as all of them sat in the kitchen eating griddlecakes and sausage, Joey noticed that Jim seemed preoccupied and had very little to say.

"What's the matter, Jim?" the boy asked. "Are you worried about something?"

"As a matter of fact, Joey, I am." Jim put down his fork and addressed Pete. "That phone call was from Fred Fowler. He's alerting all the other ranchers in the valley. His ranch was raided last night."

"No foolin'!" Pete scowled and glanced at Joey.

"Raided?" Joey asked. "What's that mean?"

"Four mares are missing from Mr. Fowler's herd," Jim explained. "He thinks they were lured away during the night by a wild horse."

"Gosh!" Joey said. "We'd better be careful of our own horses."

"That's right," Jim agreed. He pushed his coffee cup toward Pete. "Fill it up just once more. Then we'd all better buckle down and get to work. Being off the ranch yesterday put us behind schedule."

The day passed busily without further incident. And by ten everyone on the Broken Wheel Ranch was in bed and asleep.

Joey was restless during the night and awoke earlier than usual in the morning, with an odd feeling that something was wrong. He sat up in bed and peered out his west window. Fury's corral was empty! Fearfully, he leaped out of bed and ran from the room, calling Jim at the top of his voice. In a few seconds both Jim and Pete appeared in the living room.

"What's the trouble?" Pete asked.

"I don't know. Did you hear Joey calling?"

"I shore did. That's what woke me up."

Joey's shrill voice came from the porch. "*Jim!* Fury's *gone!*"

The men rushed through the door and found Joey pointing to the empty corral. "He's gone!" Joey wailed. "Where *is* he?"

The men exchanged troubled glances.

"Where's Fury?" Joey shrieked. "What happened to him?"

"Easy, Joey, easy," Jim said. "He must have jumped his corral during the night."

Joey's eyes widened in anguish. "Jumped his corral? Why would he do that?"

"I'm sure I don't know." Jim took Joey by the shoulders. "Joey, there's something Pete and I didn't tell you yesterday."

As Joey listened, not wanting to believe, Jim told him what had happened the previous morning. When Jim had finished, the boy was almost in tears.

"But Fury'll come back again, won't he, Jim? Like he did yesterday?"

"I hope he will," Jim said. "Meanwhile, let's all get some clothes on and go looking for him." He gave Joey a gentle push toward the door. "Get going."

As soon as all of them were dressed, they hurried to the stable to saddle their horses for the search. Just before they were ready to mount, Joey gave a jubilant cry and pointed toward the meadow.

"There he *is!* He's coming *back!*"

As the men turned, they saw Fury loping wearily through the entrance of the ranch. Joey gave a whoop and ran down to meet him.

"Fury!" he called. "Where have you been?"

The exhausted stallion stopped at the gate of his corral and stood with his head down, waiting to be let in. Joey arrived, breathless, and threw his arms around the grimy, sweat-covered neck. "Oh, Fury, Fury, where were you?" he moaned. "When I looked out the window and saw that you weren't here I—I didn't know what to do!"

Jim and Pete unsaddled the horses in grim silence and joined Joey at the corral. After Fury had been led inside and the gate had been closed, Pete looked at the heaving, mud-caked horse and shook his head.

"I swear I never seen a horse in such a tur'ble condition. He looks jist like a miser'ble tramp."

"Why did you do it, Fury?" Joey asked in a tremulous voice. "Jim told me you did the same thing yesterday." He looked up at Jim. "Jim—what're we gonna do with him? He might get hurt."

"That's true, he might," Jim answered seriously. "But the first thing *you're* going to do with him is clean him up. And that's going to be some job, so you'd better start in and get busy."

It took Joey several hours to get Fury back into respectable shape, and, after he had finished, his arms ached. When the bucket and other tools had been put away, he brought Jim and Pete to the corral to show them what a good job he had done. Joey climbed inside the inclosure, while the men stood beyond the fence.

As Jim and Pete were expressing their approval of Fury's appearance, a rider galloped through the ranch gate. It was Charlie Stevens. As he approached the corral, the visitor called out in alarm.

"Jim! Get that boy out of there! Do you want him to be killed by that wild stallion?"

The agitated Stevens reined up alongside of Jim and Pete.

"Fury won't harm Joey," Jim said. "You know very well Joey can handle him."

"I sure can, Mr. Stevens," Joey said, climbing over the fence.

"I'm glad *somebody* can," Stevens said indignantly.

"Whattaya mean by that?" Pete inquired, bristling.

The angry rancher glared at Fury. "*My* ranch was raided last night!"

Jim's heart skipped a beat. "I'm sorry to hear that, Charlie," he said softly.

Stevens grunted. "Being sorry isn't going to replace the six horses I lost!"

Pete scratched his chin and looked up at Stevens, quizzically. "Are you blamin' Fury fer stealin' 'em?"

"I didn't say that!" the man shot back. "But I do think that a wild horse raided my herd."

"It wasn't Fury!" Joey cried. "Fury'd never do a thing like that!"

"Wouldn't he?" Stevens said. "I happen to know that Fury jumped his corral last night."

Joey felt himself gripped by a cold, sudden fear. "How—how did you find that out?" he stammered.

"Never mind how I found it out," Stevens answered. "The man who told me knew what he was talking about."

Jim spoke up. "All right, Charlie, I admit it. Fury did break out last night, and I suppose somebody saw him. But did you actually see him raiding your place?"

"That's neither here nor there," the rancher argued. "You know as well as I do that this horse is still wild. Last time I was here, I told you he'd revert to type some day. So now he's done it; he's broken out at night."

"But, Charlie," Jim said, smiling, "when a horse is as full of energy as Fury, he's bound to break away once in a while. He's like a kid penned up in school twenty-four hours a day."

"That's no argument," Stevens said harshly. "Fury is a vicious horse. He ought to be destroyed!"

Joey gasped. He was too stunned to speak.

"Now listen here, Charlie!" Jim burst out. "You can't ride into this ranch and—"

"That's enough!" Stevens interrupted. "This horse is unmanageable! If he ever gets loose again and comes up to my ranch, I'll take care of him, myself!"

The angry rancher wheeled his horse and rode away. From his window in the bunkhouse, Bart watched

Stevens gallop through the gate, and chuckled to himself. Early that morning he had seen the empty corral, and, hoping to make trouble for Fury, had telephoned Stevens from the extension in the barn.

CHAPTER 9

The White Raider

AFTER Charlie Stevens had ridden away, Joey walked slowly to the fence of the corral and gazed at Fury in despair. For the first time since his arrival at the Broken Wheel, he felt wretched and completely alone. Seeming to sense his young master's dejection, Fury trotted to the fence and whinnied. Joey laid his cheek upon the soft muzzle. In a moment he felt Jim's comforting hand on his shoulder, and, without turning, he spoke in an agonized voice.

"You'll never let anybody kill him—will you, Jim?"

"Of course not, Joey." Jim rumpled the boy's hair. "Let's get on with the chores, shall we? There's plenty to be done."

"Sure, Jim," Joey said. After giving Fury a loving pat, he walked dejectedly up to the house.

Jim watched the troubled boy for a moment, then shook his head. "This is a serious crisis, Pete. Do you think Charlie Stevens will cool off?"

"I dunno, Jim. I reckon ya can't feel too sore at him fer feelin' the way he does. After all, Fury has been gittin' out at night, an' some blabbermouth musta seen him runnin' loose and called Charlie. An' Charlie ain't the kinda man that can lose six horses without raisin' Cain about it." Pete furrowed his brow. "Ya know, Jim, ya can hardly blame him fer thinkin' it was Fury that raided his herd."

Jim spoke sharply. "Maybe not. But Stevens really got my back up—riding in here so high and mighty and making threats. He owns the biggest spread in the valley, and he thinks he ought to own everything else that's worthwhile—including Fury." Jim turned on his heel. "Let's get to work."

For the rest of the day, Joey moved despondently about the ranch, performing his chores in silence. During the afternoon, Bart slouched into the stable to get a piece of equipment and found Joey cleaning the stalls.

"Hiya, kid," Bart said, with unaccustomed friendliness. "Hey, I seen the boss had a visitor this mornin'—that man Stevens."

Joey nodded his head and went on with his work.

Bart's mouth opened into a grin, displaying his coarse, yellow teeth. "I didn't hear what Stevens said, 'cause I was in the bunkhouse, but he looked burned-up about somethin'." Receiving no comment from Joey, the bronc-buster picked up the equipment he had come for and left the stable.

That evening, Joey skipped his usual after-supper ride on Fury. He knew that the horse needed no additional exercise after his two nights of roaming. Joey went to bed early, and after tossing and turning for a few hours, fell into a light sleep that was disturbed by troubled dreams.

Sometime after midnight, Joey was roused from his fitful slumber by sounds of nervous movement in Fury's corral. Tossing the covers aside, he leaped from his bed and ran to the window. To his dismay, in the light of the rising moon, he saw Fury just clearing the top rail of the fence.

"Fury—don't!" he pleaded half aloud. "Fury! Come back!"

Joey's heart sank as he watched Fury canter through

the ranch gate and head northward. The boy believed that if he wanted to save his beloved horse he must take matters into his own hands. He dressed hastily, but silently, so as not to awaken the others, then lowered himself from the window and dropped to the ground. In the stable he saddled Cactus, snatched up a coil of rope, and led the horse to the ranch gate before mounting him. A moment later he was riding up the valley in search of Fury.

After he had put a safe distance between himself and the ranchhouse, Joey reined in and called at the top of his voice. "Fury . . . Fu—ree!" He listened attentively, but heard no answering sound. Spurring Cactus with his heels, he continued onward.

After an hour of riding and calling Fury's name, Joey saw a hill not far ahead. Before he reached the rise, his mount snorted and threw his head up.

"What is it, Cactus?" Joey said excitedly. "Do you hear Fury?"

Cactus whinnied softly and Joey reined him in. "Fury!" he called. "Fury—do you hear me?" He listened expectantly, scanning the moonlit hill. A tremor passed through his horse's body. "He must be around here," Joey muttered. "Maybe up on that hill." His voice rose to a shout. "Fury! Are you up there?"

Suddenly Joey heard a sound, some yards ahead. Something was moving through the underbrush. The sound stopped. "Fury, is that you?" he called. "Fury —it's me—Joey!"

Then, as the boy strained his ears, listening, he heard the neigh of a horse. The sound was strange and weird, but Joey knew that it had been made by Fury. The underbrush crackled again, and soon a dark, familiar shape appeared against the sky at the top of the rise.

"Fury!" Joey cried in exultation. "Wait there! Wait for me!"

He slapped the rein, and Cactus shot forward. Upon their approach, Fury danced about nervously, alternately looking from Joey to the hollow on the opposite side of the hill. Joey rode to Fury's side and brought Cactus to a halt.

"Fury!" Joey exclaimed. "You're lucky I found you!" He took the coil of rope from his saddle horn and looped it around Fury's neck. "Don't you know what Mr. Stevens wants to do to you? He wants to shoot you! I've got to get you back to your corral before anybody knows you ran away again."

Fury snorted and jerked his head around toward the hollow. Cactus threw his ears forward, listening.

"What is it?" Joey asked. "Do you hear something down there?" Now the boy, too, heard sounds coming from down below: the sounds of horses milling about in a corral. He stood up in his stirrups and craned his neck. In the silver moonlight he saw a huge ranch, spread out over many acres. On the water tower, in large, black letters, Joey read the name: "STEVENS."

A wave of fear shot through the boy's body. "Mr. Stevens' ranch!" he gasped. "Come on—we've got to get out of here!" He sat down and pulled the rope taut, but Fury jerked back, refusing to move.

"Come on, Fury—hurry!" Joey insisted. Fury still refused to obey. Both horses were staring down at the ranch. In the corral just below them, the horses were making excited sounds. "What's going on down there?" Joey said. Rising again in his stirrups, he looked down and saw a dozen horses racing aimlessly around their inclosure.

"What's the matter with Mr. Stevens' horses?" Joey wondered aloud.

As he watched, puzzled, he suddenly saw the cause

of the disturbance. A gigantic horse had emerged from the shadows and was moving quickly to the gate of the corral. The animal was snow-white from head to tail. Fury reared in excitement, almost jerking the rope from Joey's hands. Joey kneed Cactus in closer and wound his end of the rope around the saddle horn.

"A white stallion!" he exclaimed in amazement. "So *that's* why you've been jumping your corral!"

The white horse lowered his head and seemed to be pushing the corral gate with his nose.

"What's he doing?" Joey murmured, spellbound.

A few seconds later he learned the answer. The white horse had gnawed through the rope loop which held the gate closed. The gate swung open a few feet. The white raider pushed it open still farther with his rump and bounded into the corral among the screaming horses. Nipping at them ferociously with his teeth, he drove them out through the gate.

"He's stealing them!" Joey cried. "He's stealing Mr. Stevens' horses!"

As Fury pranced about in feverish excitement, Joey watched the stolen horses race away through the night, urged on by the white raider. The theft had been committed in less than a minute. Even though he was almost overwhelmed by the sight which he had just witnessed, Joey had a feeling of tremendous relief.

"Oh, Fury!" he cried joyfully. "I knew it wasn't you that raided the ranches! It was the *white* stallion—not *you!*"

Lights were coming on, all over the Stevens ranch. Joey thought of riding down and telling Mr. Stevens about the white raider, but when he realized how angry the rancher would be, he decided to hurry back home, where Fury would have Jim's protection. He turned

Cactus around and headed south, trailing Fury at the end of the rope.

An hour and a half later, when Joey rode into the Broken Wheel, he tethered Cactus and led Fury into his corral. The runaway stallion had calmed down completely and seemed content to be back home. Both Jim and Pete had been awakened by the slamming of the corral gate, and, as the boy raced toward the house, Jim appeared on the porch in his pajamas, closely followed by Pete, clad in a long nightshirt.

"What're you doing out there?" Jim called.

"Wait'll I tell you!" Joey cried happily. "It's wonderful!" He bounded up the steps.

"What's wonderful about gittin' us up in the middle of the night?" Pete growled sleepily.

Joey was almost exploding with his news. "Mr. Stevens' ranch was raided tonight! A white stallion did it! I saw him!"

"What?" Jim said incredulously.

"You better git back to bed," Pete suggested. "You been havin' a nightmare."

"No! No!" Joey insisted. "Fury jumped his corral, and I saw him do it! I got dressed and went after him on Cactus!"

Jim glanced at Pete to observe his reaction.

"He's dressed all right," Pete muttered.

Joey poured out his story. "When I found him, he was over by Mr. Stevens' ranch. I put a rope around his neck; then I heard noises in the corral. Then I saw this white stallion open the gate and drive the horses out!"

Pete made a wry face. "You seen a horse *open* a corral gate?"

"Yes—while I was watching!" Joey turned to Jim in elation. "Jim, it isn't Fury who's been stealing those horses! It's that white stallion!"

"Hm," Jim said.

Joey saw disbelief on the men's faces. "Look, it's the truth!" he insisted.

Pete raised an eyebrow. "Mebbe so," he said doubtfully.

Joey raised his voice. "Honest! If you don't believe Fury was out, come down and look at him."

"Okay, we'll do that," Jim said. "As soon as we get some pants and shoes on. Meanwhile, you put Cactus back in his stall."

A short while later, at the corral, the men needed only to glance at Fury to know that he had been out on another journey.

"He's been travelin' somewhere," Pete observed.

"He sure has," Jim agreed. He turned to Joey. "You actually *saw* the Stevens corral being raided?"

"Yes, *sir*—right after I got the rope on Fury."

Jim sighed. "Joey—are you sure it wasn't right *before* you got the rope on Fury?"

"Yes, Jim—honest!" Joey was stung by Jim's attitude. Jim had never doubted him before.

Jim's face softened. "Joey—both Pete and I *want* to believe you. I mean that."

Joey looked at the ground. He was having a hard time keeping the tears back. Jim took him by the arm.

"Come on, son, let's go up to the house and talk some more."

As they were going up the porch steps, Pete said, "Joey, me an' Jim want to believe you more'n anything." He shook his head. "The thing that looks bad is —what was Fury doin' at Stevens' place if he didn't go to the raid?"

"I know it looks bad," Joey said with difficulty. "But don't you see? Fury went because he knew the white stallion was out on the range, somewhere."

They filed through the door into the living room.

"All I can tell you," Joey added desperately, "is that it wasn't Fury that raided the corral—it was a *white* stallion."

The telephone jangled.

"I thought so," Jim said grimly. "That'll be Stevens." He picked up the phone. "Broken Wheel Ranch, Jim Newton."

"This is Charlie Stevens!" The angry man spoke so violently, and his voice was pitched so high, that both Pete and Joey could hear his words crackling through the receiver.

"Hello, Charlie," Jim said. "What's on your—"

The voice cut in: "My ranch was raided again tonight!"

"I know."

"You *know? How* do you know?"

"Because Fury was out tonight."

"Ha!" Stevens said triumphantly. "Then I was right all along."

"Now wait a second," Jim said. "Let me tell you the story. Joey saw Fury jump his corral, saddled a horse, and rode out to bring him back. He found him near your ranch. He claims he saw a white stallion stealing your herd."

"What? Don't be ridiculous! If there was a white stallion running loose on the range, we'd know about it!"

"Well, that's the boy's story," Jim went on. "Have you found your missing horses?"

"No, we have not!" Stevens retorted. "Some of my hands and I have been out looking for them. But there's not a sign of them."

"I'm sorry, Charlie."

"Sorry? How's that going to help? Listen to me, Jim!" Stevens raged. "It's mighty funny that all of a sudden a white stallion appears, and that kid of yours is the only one who sees him. The boy's obviously lying!"

Jim bristled. "I don't like that kind of talk, Charlie! And I'm telling you not to repeat it until we've checked Joey's story. Will you give us a chance to check it?"

There was silence in the receiver for a second or two. "Okay," Stevens agreed reluctantly. "I'll give you that chance."

Jim looked relieved. "Thanks. Pete and I will start covering the range early in the morning. You want to ride with us?"

"No. I'll go out with my own boys again."

"Fair enough. I'll be calling you," Jim concluded.

There was a click as Stevens rang off. Jim turned to Pete and Joey. "I guess you heard both ends of that conversation."

"We shore did," Pete said disgustedly. "He was hollerin' so loud, he didn't even need to use a phone."

"Mr. Stevens said I was lying," Joey murmured. His eyes flashed angrily. "You'll find out that what I told you was the truth!"

Jim nodded wearily. "I hope so, Joey." He reached for the light switch. "Now let's all get to bed. Pete, in just a few hours you and I will have to be up and riding."

The two men had been in the saddle for eight hours. Finally Jim raised his hand and Pete rode up beside him and stopped.

"Any signs of horses yet?" Pete asked.

"Not one," Jim said.

The old foreman took his hat off and wiped his brow with his bandanna. "If that white stallion of Joey's is out here anywhere, he must be hidin' in a gopher hole." He heaved an exhausted sigh. "The only horses we've set eyes on are the ones we're settin' on."

"Right—and they're getting pretty tuckered."

The two men had been following the rim of a box canyon, with Jim riding in the lead. The canyon was shaped roughly like a circle, with one open end. Jim leaned out of his saddle and peered down into the canyon. It was twenty or thirty feet deep.

"No horses down there," he announced. "Let's ride north. That way we'll make a complete circle on the way back."

They clucked to their horses and moved away from the canyon's rim. For another hour they cantered along, scanning the range, having little to say to each other. As they topped a small rise, Jim straightened up and pointed. In the distance a group of three horsemen were riding toward them.

"Charlie Stevens and his men," Jim said. "Guess they've covered that part of the valley."

"Guess so," Pete agreed. "Wal—now comes the fireworks."

The three men rode up to Jim and Pete and reined in.

"Well, Jim," Stevens began sarcastically, "where's that phantom stallion the boy saw?"

"No sign of him yet, Charlie."

Stevens snorted. "Are you satisfied now?"

Jim looked the man straight in the eye. "Charlie, if Joey saw that white stallion, then he must be out here, somewhere."

Clem, one of Stevens' ranch hands, spoke up. "Man, we combed every canyon an' gulley fer ten miles around." He smirked. "But we didn't find no white horse."

"Mebbe ya didn't look hard enough!" Pete snapped.

Jim ignored the ranch hand. "Pete and I are going to keep on searching, Charlie. What about you?"

"I'm a busy man," Stevens said importantly. "And this is just a waste of my time. I'll play along with your notion for one more day—but that's all."

"Thank you," Jim said gratefully. "I can't ask for more."

"By the way," Stevens added darkly. "I'm setting up an armed patrol tonight. If we spot any horse that doesn't belong on my ranch—white or *black*—we're going to shoot him on sight."

Jim stiffened. "Now listen, Charlie—"

"I've done enough listening!" the rancher cut in. He gave a hand signal to his men, and the trio wheeled and galloped away.

Jim and Pete sat still in their saddles, watching the group of riders growing smaller. Finally, Pete slapped his saddle angrily.

"That Stevens! He must have a rock in his chest!"

"Let's forget Stevens," Jim said purposefully. "It's a long time till sundown." He kneed his horse. "Let's keep on looking."

CHAPTER 10

Death Sentence

SHADING HIS EYES from the glare of the setting sun, Joey stood in the open door of the hayloft and looked out over the valley. From that high station, he was able to scan a vast area of the range. To his disappointment, Jim and Pete were nowhere in sight. Their lateness in returning heightened Joey's suspense. It could mean that they had not even sighted the white raider and were staying out to continue their search. On the more optimistic side, their tardiness might mean that they had located their quarry and were pursuing him for a great distance. Joey could hardly control his impatience to have the men return and tell him what had actually happened.

The day that was drawing to a close had been the longest one of Joey's life. The morning hours had passed quickly enough, for he had busied himself with his chores, but the afternoon had dragged on with interminable slowness. He had climbed the ladder to the hayloft almost every hour, hoping to sight the men returning, and each fruitless trip had increased his anxiety.

Hank had been aware of the boy's apprehension and had attempted to capture his interest by giving him a lesson in rifle-shooting, but Joey had been unable to concentrate properly and had missed the tin-can targets by ridiculous margins. Hank had finally realized the wisdom of postponing the rifle practice, and Joey had thanked him and returned to his lookout in the hayloft.

The boy had been squinting into the glare for twenty minutes or more, when he finally detected a small cloud of dust in the distance. Curling the fingers of each hand, he peered through them as though they were binoculars. He was fairly sure now that he could discern two men on horseback, and he prayed that when they came closer he would see them leading a third horse—a white stallion.

When the riders reached the meadow grass, the dust cloud settled, and Joey recognized Jim and Pete—but the white stallion was not trailing behind them. He groaned in disappointment and went slowly down the ladder. As he walked from the barn into the sunlight, a sudden thought raised his spirits. Possibly the white raider had been captured and destroyed. Or perhaps Mr. Stevens and his men had taken him into custody. Eager to hear that either of these possibilities was a fact, Joey hurried to the ranch gate to meet the on-coming men. As they drew closer, it became apparent that the riders and their mounts were utterly exhausted. Jim and Pete slouched in their saddles, and the horses, their heads drooping, moved with agonizing slowness, as if every step were torture.

Joey ran toward them, shouting questions: "Did you find him? Did you capture him? Where is he? Is he dead?"

Both men shook their heads, glumly. Joey tugged at Jim's trouser leg.

"Didn't you even see him, Jim? What happened? *Tell* me!"

"Nothing happened," Jim answered wearily. "We wasted the whole day."

Joey's heart sank. The men dismounted stiffly, and

led their sweating, dust-caked horses toward the stable. Joey ran out ahead of them, then turned around and walked backward.

"Didn't you even see a sign of him?" he asked.

"Nup, not even a trace," Pete croaked.

The tired old foreman took off his grimy hat, and Joey could see a sharp line across Pete's forehead. The skin was tan above the line, and gray with dust below it. The shirts of both men were sodden and clung to their backs.

"I'm beginnin' ta think we was jest chasin' a mirage," Pete said, in a tired voice.

"But he's not a mirage!" Joey argued violently. "He's a real, live horse! I saw him!" He spoke imploringly to Jim. "You won't give up looking—will you, Jim?"

"No, Joey," Jim answered quietly. "Maybe we'll find him tomorrow."

"Oh, you will!" Joey cried. He glanced toward Fury's corral. "You've *got* to!"

"In the meantime," Jim said, prompted by Joey's glance, "let's make sure Fury stays home tonight."

"Want me to put him in a stall?" Pete asked.

"No, we'd better not risk it. If he got excited again, he'd kick a stall to pieces."

They led their footsore horses into the stable. "After supper," Jim said, "we'll get a swivel stake and a lead rope. Think that's a good idea, Pete?"

"Yeah, that oughta keep Fury home tonight."

"What do you mean?" Joey asked anxiously. "What're you going to do to Fury?"

"We're going to hammer a stake into the ground of his corral and tie him to it," Jim explained.

Joey frowned. "Tie Fury to a stake? He'll hate that!"

"I don't like it any more than he will," Jim said.

"But it's for his own good, Joey. You've got to understand that."

"Fury won't get out again tonight," Joey promised. "I'll go down to his corral and stay with him all night long."

"No, you won't—you were up all last night. You need your sleep."

"But, Jim," Joey begged. "Please don't tie him up—it would be awful!"

Jim sighed. "Joey, I wasn't going to tell you this—but now I'll have to. If Fury gets out tonight and goes up to Mr. Stevens' ranch, he'll be killed."

"*Killed?*" Joey was horrified. "How do you know?"

"Mr. Stevens told us so this afternoon." Jim looked down into the boy's ashen face and spoke earnestly. "So you see, Joey, we haven't any other choice."

Far out on the lonely range, a wild horse raced like a silver streak through the moonlight. It was the white stallion. By some freak of nature this roaming creature had become a killer, a rare phenomenon among horses. A few minutes earlier, he had been challenged by a younger stallion, which he had kicked and torn and bitten until the challenger lay dying. The smell of blood still lingered in the nostrils of the crazed white killer, and he was eager to do further battle. He thundered to the top of a butte and came to a halt. With his head erect and his tail thrown over his rump, he opened his great jaws and bugled a challenge.

At the Broken Wheel Ranch, Fury threw his ears forward and jerked his head to attention. The rope which was looped about his neck cut into the skin, causing sharp, unaccustomed pain. In an attempt to pull free of the tether he lunged backward against the unyielding rope. Again he heard the distant challenge, and again he tried to break away; but the rope held fast.

Enraged now, he tugged and strained, oblivious to the burning pain. Digging his forelegs into the ground, he threw his great weight backward against the rope, which broke just below the loop. As he fell back, his rump brushed the ground; but when he regained his footing, he dug his heels into the earth and plunged forward. Clearing the fence with ease, he galloped toward the gate and the adventure which awaited him, beyond the meadow.

Charlie Stevens was riding night guard near his main corral when he heard horsemen approaching at top speed. In a moment the men appeared, breathless and excited. They were his two ranch hands, Clem and Sam.

"Hey, Mr. Stevens!" Clem shouted as he reined in. "We come acrost one-a our horses—a young stallion that was drove out last night!"

"Where is he?" Stevens demanded.

"Layin' up there in a gulley," Sam said. "He's dead."

"*Dead?* What happened to him?"

"Looks like he was beat up by a killer horse," Clem answered. "Man, he was tore up somethin' tur'ble."

"Fury!" Stevens muttered. His face contorted with rage. "How long ago do you think it happened?"

"Couldn't-a been more'n an hour ago, by the looks of it."

Stevens slapped the stock of his rifle and spurred his mount viciously. "Come on!" he commanded. "This time we're going to get that black killer!"

Stevens was seething with anger as he and his two ranch hands thundered through the gate and headed south. They rode spread out, fifty yards apart. For twenty minutes no living thing was seen—then Clem gave a whoop.

"What is it?" Stevens shouted.

"Look!" Clem was pointing to his left.

The three men saw a dark horse racing toward a formation of high rocks. It was Fury. Stevens gave a triumphant cry and brought his mount to a sudden stop. Drawing his rifle from the saddle holster, he aimed quickly and fired. The bullet whined and pinged against the rocks. Fury reared in surprise and reversed his direction. The men rode up to Stevens and reined in.

"Ya missed him," Clem announced. A trace of derision in the man's voice enraged Stevens still further.

Fury was now racing southward, away from the men. Stevens raised his rifle and fired again. Fury continued on without faltering.

"Ya'll never touch him now," Sam said. "He's way outa range."

Stevens muttered an oath and jammed the weapon back into its holster. "A *white* stallion, huh?" he grunted. He waved his arm. "Come on, boys—he's heading back to the Broken Wheel!"

As the chase began, Fury was almost out of sight.

In the corral, Jim Newton flashed his light on the broken end of Fury's lead rope.

"Look here," he said to Joey and Pete. "Parted just below the loop."

"Took some hefty pullin' to bust that rope," Pete observed. "Fury shore musta had an awful hankerin' to leave."

Joey was distressed. "If I'd only heard him trying to get loose, maybe I could've stopped him."

Jim looked doubtful. "I don't think anybody could've stopped him. In his wild determination to get out, he must've been completely unmanageable."

In order to give medication to a sick horse, Jim had set his alarm clock for three. But before returning to the house he had dropped by the corral to check Fury's tether. Finding Fury gone, he had awakened Pete. Aroused by the commotion, Joey had slipped into his jeans and joined the men at the empty corral. He picked up the broken rope and fondled it between his hands.

"It beats me," Pete said. "Fury ain't bustin' out at night jest 'cause he's got a wild streak. He's got some kinda instinct that's makin' him do it."

Jim looked thoughtful. "You may be right, Pete, but—" He stopped short and raised his hand for silence.

As the three listened, there came the faint sound of a galloping horse.

Joey's face brightened. "Maybe it's—"

"Quiet!" Jim ordered.

The sound grew in volume, and as the three turned their heads toward the meadow, a dark, hurtling shape appeared in the moonlight.

"It *is* Fury!" Joey cried delightedly.

The boy raced to the gate to meet his returning friend. Seeing Joey waiting, Fury slowed down to a trot and lowered his head. The loop of rope still encircled his neck, and Joey grasped it with both hands.

"Fury, Fury—where have you been?"

Fury's sides were heaving, and his muzzle was covered with foam. Jim hurried to Joey's side, took the rope, and returned Fury to his corral. As on the previous night, the horse seemed content to be home again.

While the men were examining Fury's legs and Joey was fondling his head, the sound of riders reached their ears. As they looked up, Stevens and his two men approached the gate and entered it, riding hard. Jim, Pete, and Joey left Fury and met the mounted men at the fence. Stevens' voice was thunderous.

"Now don't tell me that horse has been here in the

corral all night! We just chased him the whole length of the valley!"

Jim spoke frankly. "He's been out, Charlie, we won't deny it."

"You'd better not!"

Jim's two bronc-busters came from the bunkhouse, dressed in pajama tops and trousers.

"What's all the ruckus?" Bart asked.

"Fury was out agin tonight," Pete answered.

"He certainly was!" Stevens boomed. "He killed one of my young stallions!"

"He shore as heck did," Clem added. "Cut him all up with his teeth an' his hoofs."

"It wasn't Fury!" Joey exclaimed. "Fury wouldn't do a thing like that!"

"You keep out of this!" Stevens snapped. He glared down at Jim. "Just like I've been telling you, that horse is a killer. There's no use waiting any longer to have him destroyed."

Joey cried out in anguish. *"No!* Don't *say* that!"

Jim took the boy by the arm. "Joey—go on up to the house."

"But, Jim!" He looked appealingly up into the tall man's eyes.

"You heard what I said. Go to the house."

The miserable boy hesitated for a moment, searching Jim's face, not comprehending his sudden sternness.

"Go on, Joey," Jim said firmly. "Do as I say."

Tears welled up into Joey's eyes and spilled down on his cheeks. With a last, despairing look at Fury, he climbed through the fence and ran to the house.

"Well, Jim," Stevens said gruffly, "now that that's over, what've you got to say?"

Jim raised his arms in a gesture of finality. "I'm convinced. Fury will be destroyed."

"It's about time," Stevens said. "You going to do it?"

Jim shook his head. "I'll get Doc Weathers out here in the morning."

Stevens shrugged. "Okay—as long as the job gets done. Personally, I think you're out of your mind to pay a vet to put that killer away." He slapped the stock of his rifle. "Why not be sensible and use one of these?"

Jim winced. "I couldn't do it, Charlie."

"*I'll* do it, boss," a gruff voice announced.

All heads turned toward the speaker. It was Bart, who had been listening with a crooked grin on his face.

"It won't bother me none ta shoot him," Bart went on. "I got a rifle up at the bunkhouse. I'll put a slug in that killer's skull an' save ya the vet's fee."

Jim didn't answer. Bart hesitated, then turned away and started eagerly for the bunkhouse. "I'll git my rifle an' be right back," he called.

Jim snapped an order. "Hold it, Bart!"

The bronc-buster stopped and looked back. "Huh?"

"Fury isn't going to be shot," Jim said resolutely. "Doc Weathers will take care of him the humane way."

Bart threw up his hands and slouched away, grumbling.

Stevens spoke up. "Jim, you were foolish to turn down Bart's offer to help. He's a good, trustworthy man. He'd do a nice, clean job for you."

Jim glared at the rancher and spoke with deadly, deliberate calm. "You heard me, Charlie—Doc Weathers will take care of it in the morning. That's final."

Stevens shrugged. "Okay, have it your way. I'll drop over in the morning, myself."

"What for?"

"To make sure that Doc Weathers does the job

properly." Stevens wheeled his horse. "Let's go, boys."

After the three men had ridden through the gate, Jim stole a glance at Pete, who had been silent for a long time. The old foreman looked tired and careworn. Jim moved slowly to the fence and draped his arms wearily over the top rail. Pete trailed after him and spoke in a low, husky voice.

"Jim—did ya see the look on Joey's face?"

Jim nodded. "Of course I did."

Pete stared, saying nothing. Suddenly, Jim stood erect and pounded the rail with his fist.

"What else can I do? I tried hard to believe! I tried as hard as I could!"

"I know—so did I." Pete laid his hand on Jim's shoulder. "I think mebbe ya oughta go up an' have a talk with him." His voice broke. "I—I reckon he's purty miser'ble."

"Yes," Jim said huskily. "I reckon he is."

The tall, troubled man climbed the fence and walked toward the house.

CHAPTER 11

The Battle

AFTER the ranchhouse had become dark and silent, Joey slipped out of bed and tiptoed quietly to the window. Fury was standing helpless in the corral, tethered and hobbled. This time Pete had done a thorough job; he had driven three stakes into the ground, in the form of a triangle with twenty-foot sides. Fury was in the center of the triangle, with a separate rope extending from his neck to each stake. In addition, he wore a hobble on his forelegs.

As Joey looked out at the immobilized horse, his heart filled with pity for the innocent prisoner, who had been accused of crimes which he had not committed and who had been unjustly condemned to death.

Jim's heart-to-heart talk with Joey had not lessened the boy's despair. On the contrary, it had led to even greater melancholy and frustration. Jim had attempted to comfort him by explaining how Fury would be dispatched painlessly. He had said that Doc Weathers would give the horse something that would put him to sleep and that Fury would never know what happened. When Joey had hysterically repeated his argument that the white horse, not Fury, was to blame for the raids and the killing, Jim had become stern again and had left the room.

As he gazed out the window at the fettered horse,

Joey was numbed by a feeling of utter hopelessness. He alone knew of the existence of the white stallion. If only someone would believe him, Fury would be saved—but no one would believe him, not even Jim.

"Just because I'm a kid," Joey moaned, "they all think I'm lying. Nobody likes Fury any more except me—and I don't count."

His voice caught in his throat, and tears ran down his cheeks. Burying his face in his arms, he gave way to uncontrolled sobbing. Presently he heard a strange, forlorn sound in the corral. Fury was making low, distressed noises in his throat, as though he, too, were weeping. The piteous moaning was more than Joey could bear, and he felt that he must go to the corral and put a stop to it. He moved from the window and began to dress hurriedly. While he was getting into his jeans, a bold plan leaped into his mind. It was a wild scheme, absolutely fantastic, but Joey believed that it might work. It *had* to work, he decided—it was Fury's only chance.

Leaving the house by the bedroom window, the boy crept stealthily to the stable, saddled Cactus, and led the faithful horse to the ranch gate, where he tied the bridle to a post. Returning furtively to the corral, he slipped through the fence and began to remove the loops from Fury's neck. The delighted horse nuzzled Joey's shoulder and whinnied happily.

"Quiet, Fury!" Joey murmured, while loosening the ropes. "If you wake up Jim and Pete, it'll spoil everything. The way they've got you tied up, no wonder you were feeling so bad. If you could only talk you'd tell them about that white horse, and then they'd have to believe me." Fury was free now, except for the hobble on his forelegs. He was trembling violently. "Listen," Joey whispered excitedly, "even if you can't talk, maybe you can show me where to find the white

stallion." He crouched down and removed the hobble. Fury looked eagerly toward the range. "Okay,
Fury," Joey said, leaping up. "Find him! Take me to
him!"

He gave Fury a sharp slap on the rump. The horse
shot forward, leaped the fence, and bolted toward the
ranch gate. Joey snaked through the bars, hurried to
the waiting Cactus, untied him, and vaulted into the
saddle. Fury was already a hundred yards out on the
range, heading toward the hills.

"Let's go, Cactus!" Joey commanded. "Run!"

Once he was safely out of earshot of the ranch,
Joey called to Fury at the top of his voice. "Fury, wait!
Wait for me!"

At first, Fury paid no attention to Joey's repeated
cries, but finally he stopped running and looked back,
pawing the ground impatiently. As the boy drew
near on his galloping horse, Fury turned and raced
ahead again.

Hours later, when the first rays of morning light
glistened on the dewdrops, the steaming horses and
the exhausted boy were high in the hills, still searching
for the white killer.

When Jim burst into the kitchen, Pete was cooking
breakfast.

"Where's Joey?" Jim demanded.

Pete jumped. "Ya scared me, dang it!"

"Never mind that. Have you seen him?"

"No. Ain't he in bed?"

"No!"

Pete turned a strip of bacon. "Then mebbe he's out in
the corral with Fury."

"He's not." Jim strode to the window. "Fury's gone,
too."

"What?" Pete dropped his fork with a clatter. "That's impossible! I had him hobbled an' triple-staked!"

"He didn't break away—he was freed."

Pete's jaw fell. "Joey done it!"

Jim nodded and punched the wall angrily.

"Pore kid," Pete said. "I reckon he didn't wanta wait fer Doc Weathers."

Jim's face grew grim. "Pete, he could be in real trouble." He turned and hurried out. "Let's get saddled up. We've got to go and find him."

Pete turned off the stove and followed Jim out. Within a few minutes they were ready to ride. As they were leaving the stable, Pete pointed disgustedly toward the gate.

"Dang it—we got comp'ny!"

Charlie Stevens had ridden through the gate, followed by his two ranch hands. Jim and Pete cantered toward them.

" 'Morning," Stevens called harshly.

Jim nodded. "Good morning, Charlie—boys."

The visitors reined in. In the empty corral they saw the ropes tied to the swivel stakes.

Stevens scowled. "Has Doc Weathers been here already?"

"No," Jim answered impatiently. "Both Joey and Fury are missing."

"Missing?" Stevens shook his finger in Jim's face. "Now listen to me! If you think stalling's going to make me change my mind, you've got another think coming!"

Jim ran out of temper. "Stop it, Charlie!" he shouted. "Stop talking for a change and listen to *me!*"

Stevens and his men exchanged surprised glances.

"I've had just about enough out of you!" Jim continued hotly. "That boy might be in danger, and all you can think of is your petty revenge!"

Stevens turned lobster red. "Revenge?"

"Yes, revenge!" Jim lowered his voice, but spoke with furious intensity. "Now you and your men can do one of two things—either turn your horses around and high-tail it off my ranch or ride out and help us look for Joey!"

Stevens hesitated, realizing that Jim was deadly serious.

"Well?" Jim demanded. "Which will you do?"

Stevens glowered. "Okay, Jim, we'll ride along and help you look. But remember," he added threateningly, "when we find the boy—we also find the horse!"

"We'll cross that bridge when we come to it," Jim said. He barked orders to the two ranch hands: "Clem —you and Sam ride the range to the south. Charlie— you and Pete and I will search the canyon country!"

Jim spurred his horse and led the procession to the gate. Once outside, the five men separated into two groups, which rode in opposite directions.

By eleven o'clock the sun was unbearably hot, and Joey was burning with thirst. Fury had led him through rough, rocky country, but now he was riding among tall cedars, growing so closely together that the branches whipped his face. Finally, to the delight of both Joey and Cactus, they came to a clearing beside the bank of a small stream. Fury was out of sight by this time, but Joey slid to the ground and stretched prone on the bank. After soaking his head, he began to drink the cool water. Cactus moved further down the stream and walked into it, where he stood in the water up to his knees, noisily sucking up great drafts.

After Joey had drunk his fill and was bathing his arms, he heard a crashing behind him among the cedars. Cactus threw his head up, with his muzzle dripping, and uttered a frightened squeal.

Joey raised himself to his knees and called: "Fury
. . . Fury—is that you?"

Cactus splashed hurriedly to the opposite bank and
dashed into the woods, bawling in terror.

"Cactus!" Joey cried. "Come back here!"

The crashing behind Joey grew louder, and as he
scrambled to his feet and whirled around, a wild-eyed
horse emerged from among the trees. It was the white
killer stallion! His mane was matted with burrs and
twigs, and his hide was splotched with dried blood.
Seeing Joey, he bared his teeth and made vicious
sounds.

Alarmed by the maddened animal, Joey stepped
backward and fell full-length into the stream. The
white killer uttered a wild cry and stomped his hoofs
on the bank. Joey flipped over and scrambled through
the water on all fours.

"Fury!" he screamed. "Fury—help!"

The crazed horse plunged into the stream and ad-
vanced upon the fleeing boy.

"Fury!" Joey screamed again. *"Fury!"*

From downstream came Fury's answer. It was a
deep-throated cry, which reverberated through the
forest—a trumpet challenge—the battle cry of the
fighting stallion.

The white killer jerked his head up and contemptuously bawled his defiance of the challenger. He
was spoiling for battle—he welcomed it eagerly and
boldly. Hearing the sound of approaching hoofbeats,
the white whirled to face his enemy. In a moment
Fury thundered into view. He was galloping through
the stream bed, sending up a curtain of spray.

Screaming with rage, the two stallions met in mid-
stream. Both reared to their hind legs and struck out
with their forefeet. With bared teeth, they sought each
other's throats.

Joey staggered to the bank and watched the battle, tense with fear and excitement, yet horrified by the thought that Fury might be killed by his mad antagonist. He knew that when two enraged stallions met in combat, it was often a battle to the death.

Less than a mile away, Jim's searching party heard Fury's challenge to the white killer. Roweling their horses, they changed direction and raced toward the scene of battle. They rode with their heads low, but their faces were lashed by the thick, overhanging branches. As they sped along, the screams of the fighting stallions reached their ears. When they were still some distance from the conflict, they saw movement among the trees ahead, and presently Cactus came running toward them, his eyes wild with fear.

"It's Cactus!" Pete cried.

Jim saw the empty saddle and was horror-struck. As the terrified horse swept by, Pete reached out to grasp his dangling rein.

"Never mind him!" Jim shouted. "Let's find Joey!"

As the riders plunged on, the battle cries of the stallions stopped suddenly. The men reined in.

"Joey!" Jim called. "Joey!"

"Jim!" The boy's voice was faint and far-off.

"Where are you?" Jim cried.

"Down here! Come quick! It's the white stallion!"

The men slapped their reins and galloped toward the sound of the boy's voice.

"Are you all right?" Jim shouted.

"Yes, but hurry! He'll get away!"

The riders crashed into the clearing beside the bank of the stream. Joey was standing in the water with both arms around Fury's neck. Blood was oozing from a slash in one of Fury's heaving sides. Joey pointed excitedly upstream.

"Look! Look!"

The defeated white killer was just disappearing around a bend. Stevens slipped his rifle from the holster, took aim and fired. The horse crashed ahead, apparently unwounded.

"Put that dern thing away," Pete said disgustedly. "Unless it shoots around corners."

Jim rode into the water, leaped down, and took Joey in his arms.

"Joey," he said tenderly, "are you hurt?"

"No, I'm okay." He grinned happily. "Jim! Fury fought him—and he *licked* him!"

Fury raised his head high and trumpeted a cry of victory.

"Atta boy, Fury—you tell him!" Joey shouted.

Jim grasped Fury's mane and led him from the water. Joey followed them to the bank, splashing joyously.

Pete and Stevens were examining the wound in Fury's side.

" 'T aint bad," Pete said. "Be healed in no time at all."

Stevens reached out and patted Fury's nose. "This is quite a horse you've got here, Joey. Yes, sir-ee, quite a horse."

Jim put his hand on Joey's shoulder. "Joey," he said earnestly, "I hope you'll forgive us. Will you?"

"Sure, Jim," Joey said. "Pete, too."

Jim looked at Stevens. "I mean *all* of us, Joey."

The boy turned to Stevens and frowned. The man's eyes were moist as he waited imploringly for Joey to speak. Finally, when no words were forthcoming, Stevens knelt down on one knee and took the silent boy by the shoulders.

"Joey," he said huskily, "I'm not asking you to forgive me—I'm *begging* you."

Joey grinned. "Okay, Mr. Stevens—I guess we all make mistakes."

Stevens gathered Joey into his arms and hugged him. "Thank you, son," he whispered. "Thank you."

CHAPTER 12

A Voice from the Dead

DURING the remainder of the summer, the ranchers of the valley watched constantly for the white killer stallion, but to everyone's satisfaction he seemed to have departed from the locality. From time to time, he was reported to have been seen on other ranges in surrounding states, but the rumors were never verified, and no one ever succeeded in capturing him. Finally, the white raider became almost legendary, like "The Ghost of the Staked Plain" of the 1870's.

By the middle of September, Joey had become so proficient at ranch work that Jim and Pete wondered how they had ever managed the operation without the boy's help. Secretly, both men dreaded the imminent reopening of the valley school, for Jim had developed a deep, fatherly love for his adopted son, and Pete had become a typical doting uncle.

For Joey, the summer had been glorious, but he looked forward eagerly to a reunion with his classmates. Fury had become a genuine hero since his defeat of the killer stallion, and Joey could hardly be blamed for anticipating the proud pleasure of riding his four-footed celebrity to school.

On the first day of the fall term, Helen Miller, the pleasant young teacher, took her class to the grove where the horses were tethered and invited Joey to relate the story of his and Fury's encounter with the white raider. When the tale had been told, and Joey had answered the scores of excited questions which had been hurled at him, Miss Miller returned her class to the schoolroom, and the process of learning began in earnest.

One afternoon, in the middle of the second week of the term, the valley bus stopped at the end of the lane leading up to the schoolhouse and discharged a male passenger. As the bus pulled away, the man set his battered suitcase on the ground and looked toward the front door of the school. After checking his watch, he sat down on the suitcase and lighted a cigarette.

A few moments later, Miss Miller glanced from her classroom window and noticed the waiting man. She could see he was about forty years of age, short and slight, and dressed neatly in gray trousers, a tight-fitting brown jacket, and a brown felt hat. Although the young teacher did not recognize the stranger, she assumed he was waiting for one of her students, and so dismissed him from her mind.

When the session ended, and the children ran chattering from the building, the man stood up and looked intently at each boy as he came toward him. A number of the children pedaled away on bicycles; some rode off on their horses; others walked to the bus stop to wait for transportation.

Peewee Jenkins, who had not ridden his horse to school that day, was among the group which came down to the bus stop. The stranger addressed him pleasantly.

"Excuse me, young man."

"Yes, sir?"

"Is there a boy named Joey in your class—the boy who lives at the Newton Ranch?"

Peewee grinned. "There sure is. He's one of my best friends."

"Really? Would you mind pointing him out to me?"

Peewee turned and looked back. "There he is," he said. "He's talking to that boy over there with the bike."

"Thanks a lot, son."

The man picked up his suitcase and walked toward Joey.

"So long, Bob," Joey called, as the other boy mounted his bike and rode away. As Joey started to walk back toward the grove, the man hailed him.

"Joey—just a minute."

Joey turned in surprise. "Me?"

"Yes," the man said amiably. "Aren't you Joey Clark, Junior?"

Joey frowned. "Well—yes, sir—Clark used to be my name, but now I'm Joey Newton." Joey was perplexed. "I don't understand what you mean by 'Junior.' "

The man put down his suitcase and smiled. "It means that you were named after your father." He hesitated, peering into Joey's face. "Didn't anybody ever tell you that?"

Joey thought a moment. "N-no, sir, I don't think so. You see—I never knew my father."

The man's face grew long. "I know," he said regretfully. "That was a great misfortune."

Helen Miller, who had noticed the stranger talking to her pupil, felt that it was her duty to learn his identity. She walked across the lawn and greeted him pleasantly.

"Good afternoon. I'm Joey's teacher, Miss Miller."

The man removed his hat. "Oh—how do you do?"

"Joey, do you know this gentleman?" Miss Miller asked.

"No, ma'am. He just came up to me and—"

"I was just about to introduce myself," the man interrupted. "My name is Joseph Clark—Senior."

The teacher was amazed. *"Senior?* You mean you're Joey's father?"

"That's right." Mr. Clark put his arm around Joey's shoulders. The stunned boy looked up at him.

"But—you can't be," he faltered. "My father's dead."

Clark shook his head sadly. "That's what you've been told, Joey."

Noticing Joey's expression of shocked bewilderment, Miss Miller took his hand, sympathetically. "That's what everyone has been told, Mr. Clark."

The man nodded. "I know. That was the way I wanted it—at first." He shook his head, regretfully. "It was a grave mistake."

Joey looked up at his teacher, forlornly. "What will Jim say?" he murmured.

Helen gave the boy's hand a comforting squeeze. "Mr. Clark," she said questioningly, "I suppose you know about Jim Newton?"

"Of course."

"Well—have you spoken to *him?*"

"Not yet. I wanted to see Joey first. Then I thought I'd go back to the ranch with him and meet Mr. Newton." Clark patted Joey's shoulder, affectionately. "Before talking to Mr. Newton I wanted to make the acquaintance of my boy—the son I haven't seen for so many years." He smiled down at Joey. "What do you say, son? Shall we go to the ranch together?"

"We—we can't go together," Joey answered brokenly. "I'm riding Fury—my horse."

Clark grinned. "Oh, yes—I've heard all about Fury. I'm proud of you, son. Fury must be a splendid mount."

Joey nodded vehemently. "He's the best horse in the whole world."

The teacher made a sudden decision. "If you'll wait just a moment, Mr. Clark," she suggested, "I'll lock up the school and drive you to the Broken Wheel Ranch in my car. Joey, you can follow on Fury."

"That's very kind of you, Miss Miller," Clark said agreeably. "The sooner I present myself to Mr. Newton, the better."

Mr. Clark's sudden appearance was as great a shock to Jim Newton and Pete as it had been to Joey. According to the records, both at the Children's Home and at the County Courthouse, Joey's father had been missing for more than twelve years. When Helen Miller drove Clark into the ranch and introduced him as Joey's father, both Jim and Pete were seized with a sudden, unpleasant foreboding. Without mentioning their fears to each other, the two men realized at once that the arrival of Joey's real father might mean that the boy would be taken away from them.

While waiting in the living room for Joey to return on Fury, Helen and Jim engaged Clark in polite conversation. They learned that the man's home was in Kansas City and that he worked as a salesman for a company that manufactured leather goods. Clark asked many questions about Joey's life on the ranch and seemed pleased that the boy had become such an excellent horseman.

"It doesn't surprise me, though," he said. "Joey must have inherited his love and understanding of horses from me. Twenty years ago—before I married Anne—that was Joey's mother—I worked on a Colorado ranch for a few seasons."

"Is that so?" Jim remarked politely. Although he hoped that Clark had come to the valley merely to visit Joey—not to claim him—Jim wished desperately that the man would end the suspense by coming to the point and stating the actual purpose of his visit.

Miss Miller, too, was impatient for Clark to declare himself. Well aware of the fact that Joey's true home was the Broken Wheel Ranch, she dreaded the possibility of his being uprooted and taken away by this stranger.

When Joey finally arrived, he greeted Jim gloomily and took a seat by the window. When Jim asked him if he had been pleased to learn that his real father was alive, Joey nodded dejectedly but remained silent. After a few moments of self-conscious small talk, Clark slapped his thighs with his hands and broke the tension.

"Well, Joey," he announced cheerfully, "I've got good news for you. I'm taking you back to Kansas City to live."

Joey gasped and looked at Jim, terrified. Miss Miller uttered a sharp cry and put her hand to her mouth. Jim made no sound, but his face had turned white.

Noticing their reactions, Clark was quickly apologetic. "I'm sorry," he began. "I suppose I shouldn't have been quite so blunt but—well—I'm a direct man and believe in getting to the point." He looked at Joey. "After all, Joey, I *am* your father." He hesitated, then continued in a soft, pleading voice. "Doesn't that mean anything to you?"

Joey rose from his chair and walked quickly to the doorway, where he stood looking out at Fury, who was in the far corner of the corral, switching his tail. Without turning, Joey listened apprehensively, to hear what Jim would say.

"Mr. Clark," Jim began, in a strained voice, "it must be obvious to you that your sudden announcement came as a shock to us."

"Yes, Mr. Newton, and as I said, I'm sorry. Matters of this kind are always shocking." Clark searched Jim's troubled face. "But put yourself in my place. What would you do if Joey were *your* son?"

Jim rose and held up a restraining hand. "I've thought of that. I know very well how you feel." He pounded the desk with his fist. "It's just that—well— I foolishly assumed that you were dead."

Clark smiled wryly. "Well—I for one am darn glad I'm not."

It was now Jim's turn to be apologetic. He placed a hand on Clark's shoulder. "Please forgive me. I didn't mean that the way it sounded."

Miss Miller spoke up. "I know what Jim meant, Mr. Clark. And I understand his feelings. He's made a home here for Joey, and I'm sure he loves Joey just as much as you do." She looked steadily at Clark and added, "Perhaps even more than you do."

Clark spoke calmly. "More than I do? I doubt that, Miss Miller. Joey's my own flesh and blood."

Jim now had his feelings under control. "I've adopted the boy legally," he said. "Did you know that?"

"Of course," Clark replied. "But the decree is merely temporary." He took a sheaf of papers from his pocket. "Judge Morris has revoked his decree and given me an order restoring Joey to my custody."

Jim winced and held out his hand. "Let's have a look at it."

Clark slipped a document from among the papers and handed it to Jim, who opened it and spread it out on the desk. Helen Miller rose and joined Jim in examining the Judge's signed order.

After a moment of study, Jim shook his head gravely. "I don't know much about the law," he muttered, "but this looks pretty final, doesn't it?"

Miss Miller sighed and nodded.

Clark handed over the other papers, one by one. "By way of identification," he said, "here's my marriage certificate, a photostat of Joey's birth certificate, and my honorable discharge from the service. Look them over."

"Thanks," Jim said, "I'll do that."

Clark laid a hand on Jim's arm. "Mr. Newton, I want you to know that I deeply appreciate everything you've done for my boy. I only wish that I'd made this decision last spring, before you came into the picture. It would have saved you a great deal of heartache."

"It certainly would," Jim said quietly.

"But when you took Joey into your home," Clark continued, "you did a truly fine thing."

Jim made a helpless gesture. Clark turned toward Joey, who was still standing quietly in the doorway, looking out.

"Joey," Clark said, in a tone of deep sincerity, "I know it's difficult for you to understand how your own father could have stayed away all this time. And now that I look at you, and see what a fine boy you are, I wonder myself how I could have done it." He sighed deeply. "I've missed some wonderful years with you."

Both Helen Miller and Jim were affected by the wistfulness in the man's voice. As they watched, sympathetically, Clark took a small photograph from his wallet and walked to the doorway.

"Joey," he said in a low voice, "I'd like you to look at this picture."

Joey turned, reluctantly. "What is it?" he asked.

"You don't remember her—but it's your mother." There were tears in the man's eyes as he held up the faded likeness for Joey to see. Suddenly, Joey whirled, angrily.

"I don't want to look at it!" he cried. "I never knew her—and I never knew you, either!"

"Joey!" Jim said, reprovingly.

"I don't care!" Joey shouted. "What if he is my father? He left me, didn't he? He got rid of me when I was a baby and ran away!"

"But, son," Clark said in a distressed voice. "I'm terribly sorry for what I did to you. I made a mistake and lived to regret it. But now we're going to start over, just you and I. We'll begin a new life together, as father and son."

Joey burst into tears and ran to Jim's side. "Please, Jim! Please don't make me go away with him! I want *you* to be my father—not *him!*"

Joey's teacher closed her eyes and turned away, sorrowfully. Jim took Joey gently by the shoulders.

"But don't you see?" he argued. "You've found your real father."

"No!" Joey sobbed. "You're my father!" He put his arms around Jim's waist. "Oh, Jim—you're the only father I ever want!"

Jim spoke with difficulty. "Joey, Joey, you've got to understand. The law is strict about things like this, don't you see? It demands a long waiting period before its decision is final. And when a boy's real father turns up, it's something altogether different. Mr. Clark is your real father, and his rights come first. We can't interfere with them."

Joey shook his head in violent disagreement. Jim looked imploringly to Miss Miller, who took Joey's hand and spoke softly, consolingly.

"Joey dear, maybe you'll feel differently about it after a while. In fact, I'm sure you will." She wiped

Joey's eyes with her handkerchief. "There isn't a boy in the world who doesn't want his real father."

Clark smiled gratefully. "Thank you, Miss Miller, for helping Joey to understand." He sighed. "But I wish I had time to get him to know me better before we leave here—time for him to overcome his shock and natural resentment."

"Must you leave right away?" Jim asked.

"Well, no, Mr. Newton, there's no hurry but—" He hesitated.

"All right then," Jim said. "Let's see—this is Wednesday. I'd be happy to have you stay here at the ranch till Saturday, or even longer. During that time, you and Joey can get better acquainted."

Clark shook his head, doubtfully. "That's terribly generous of you, but it seems to me we Clarks have already imposed on your hospitality."

"We'd be happy to have you," Jim insisted. "Won't you stay?"

Clark looked at Helen. "You'd better help me to decide, Miss Miller. What shall I do?"

"I think you'd better stay," she advised. "You and Joey not only can get to know each other, but he could also finish out his week at the school."

"All right, then," Clark decided. "Mr. Newton, I'd be more than happy to accept your invitation."

"That's fine."

Clark turned to Joey. "I think it's a good idea, son, don't you? Who knows—by Saturday you and I might be great pals. What do you say?" he added hopefully. "Shall we give it a try?"

"Okay," Joey murmured.

Realizing that he had only three more days to spend with Fury, the heartsick boy left the house and walked miserably out to the corral.

After Helen Miller had driven away, Clark told Jim

about a home that he was attempting to buy for Joey and himself, and asked permission to make a long-distance call to the realtor in Kansas City. Jim allowed him to make the call in private. After it had been completed, Clark went down to the corral to ask Joey to show him around the ranch.

Meanwhile, Jim had decided to ask Judge Morris' personal opinion on the restoration order, and after having made certain that Clark was safely out of ear-shot, he telephoned the county courthouse and asked to speak to the judge. To his disappointment, he was told that Judge Morris was out of town and would not return until sometime Saturday afternoon.

With a sigh, Jim hung up and leaned wearily back in his chair. With Joey gone, he thought, the Broken Wheel Ranch would be meaningless and empty.

CHAPTER 13

Mac

WHEN Jim told Pete the news about their losing Joey, the old fellow was crushed. His shoulders sagged and he seemed to age ten years in an instant. In an attempt to conceal his bitter sorrow, he shuffled into his bedroom and closed the door. A short while later, sensing that Pete might feel like talking, Jim knocked gently on the door and entered the room. Pete was lying on the bed, staring up at the ceiling.

"It jest can't be, Jim," he moaned. "This tur'ble thing jest can't happen to us."

"I know," Jim said quietly. "It doesn't seem possible. But it's going to happen, Pete. There's nothing we can do about it. It's the law."

Some of Pete's old fire returned. He slapped the mattress angrily and sat up. "The law!" he growled. "What does that Jedge Morris know about people's *feelin's?*"

"Plenty. He deals with people every day in his courtroom."

"Rats!" Pete snapped. "He deals with people all right, but what do they end up with? Fines an' jail sentences!" He sprang from the bed and paced the floor, ranting. "Jedge Morris—phooey! Dang it, Jim, —if I had my way I'd go to Washin'ton, D.C., an' take it up with the Soo-preme Court!"

Despite his depression, Jim was forced to smile at

the sight of the wiry little man stomping around the room in his stocking feet. And his mental picture of Pete arguing his case before the highest court in the land amused him even more.

Pete whirled on Jim. "How long's this Clark feller gonna stay here?" he demanded.

"Until Saturday."

"Does that mean I gotta cook meals fer him all that time?"

"Certainly, he's our guest."

Pete scratched his gray stubble thoughtfully.

"What're you thinking about?" Jim asked.

"I'm thinkin' about rat poison, that's what I'm thinkin' about! Mebbe I can slip some of it into that feller's soup tonight!"

"Now hold on," Jim said soberly. "Clark is Joey's father, and we must treat him with respect."

"Respect my Aunt Matilda!" Pete said scornfully. He pointed a finger at Jim. "Did he have any respect fer Joey all these years?"

Jim inclined his head. "You've got a point there, Pete. But the law's on his side, and no matter how we feel about it he's going to take Joey to Kansas City."

"Yeah, yeah," Pete said impatiently, "you told me all that stuff. But now tell me this—where're they gonna live when they *git* to Kansas City—in a tent?"

"No, Clark told me he's making a deal to buy a nice little house in the suburbs. In fact he made a long-distance call to the real estate company a few minutes ago. He gave them this address, so they can send him some final papers for me to look at. They should get here in Saturday morning's mail."

Pete was not impressed. "A nice little house in the suburbs, huh? Wal, all I can say is—I hope the dang little house gits struck by lightnin'!"

Jim grinned. "Then Joey and his father *would* have

to live in a tent." Something outside the window caught Jim's eye and he pulled the curtain aside. "Look out there," he said. "Joey's got his father riding Cactus. He rides well, too."

Pete looked out the window and snorted. "I wisht that was a real cactus he's settin' on, 'stead of a horse."

Jim laughed. "Well, Pete, I came in here to snap you out of your depression, and I think I succeeded. You're as ornery and sassy as you ever were, and I'm glad to see it." He slapped Pete on the back. "Now come on—jump into your boots and help me clean out those feed troughs before supper."

Although Joey was unhappy at the prospect of leaving the Broken Wheel, he was a sensible boy and realized that he would have to accept the inevitable. On Friday afternoon he said good-by to Miss Miller and his classmates and rode Fury home from school for the last time. In order to make the ride last longer, he decided to take the long way around and enter the ranch from the wooded section to the east.

As he reached the edge of the ranch property, Joey was surprised to see Mr. Clark on the trail ahead. Clark was mounted on Cactus, and talking to a burly stranger. When the men saw Joey approaching, the stranger hurried off into the woods. Clark slapped his rein and rode to meet Joey.

"Hi, son," he called genially, as the two horses came together. "I rode out to meet you on your way home from school."

"Why did you ride up this way?" Joey asked. "I almost always come in through the gate."

Clark hesitated for a fraction of a second. "I realize that," he said slowly, "but—well—I just had a hunch you might be coming this way today." He clucked to his horse. "Come on, son, let's ride down together."

As they started away, Joey turned in his saddle and looked back. "Who was that man you were talking to just now?"

Clark seemed confused. "Uh—man?"

"Sure. When he saw me coming, he went off into the woods."

"Oh, *that* man." Clark shrugged. "I don't know who he was. As I was riding along, he hailed me and asked for a cigarette." He changed the subject. "You know, Joey, this stallion of yours is the finest horse I've ever seen."

Joey was pleased, as he always was when Fury was praised. By the time he and Clark arrived at the corral, Joey had forgotten about the stranger in the woods.

It was Saturday morning—the beginning of Joey's last day at the Broken Wheel. Clark had decided that he and Joey would depart early in the afternoon, and Jim had offered to drive them into town.

Immediately after breakfast, Joey collected the currying tools from the stable and carried them down to Fury's corral. He planned to ride over to the Jenkins ranch early in the afternoon to say a last farewell to his friend Peewee, and he wanted Fury to look bright and shining.

When the mail was delivered, Jim was in the tool shed, repairing the generator. After skimming through the envelopes, he walked outside and called Clark, who was in his bedroom, packing.

"Here's your letter from Kansas City," Jim said, as Clark approached the tool shed.

Clark looked pleased. "It came right on schedule, didn't it?" He examined the envelope. "It's from the real estate company, all right."

As he was about to open the letter, he noticed Jim

looking toward the corral. Jim was shaking his head, sadly.

"You feel pretty bad about Joey, don't you?" Clark said.

Jim smiled, wanly. "I sure do." He cleared his throat. "By the way—Joey hasn't confided much in me these past few days, but do you think he's learned to accept you a little better?"

Clark shook his head. "He accepts me, I think, but that's about as far as it goes. He certainly hasn't displayed any affection for me. You know, Jim, I feel sorry for the boy—and I feel sorry for you, too. Since I've been here, I've come to understand the deep feeling that you have for each other. It makes me feel rather guilty."

Jim didn't answer. He was watching Joey, who was standing close to the fence, brushing Fury's mane with great care. Clark followed Jim's gaze. Joey had put the brush down and was stroking Fury's muzzle.

"Poor little tyke," Clark said. "Leaving Fury must be a terrible wrench for him." He put the letter in his pocket, unopened. "Jim, I think I'll walk down and see if I can comfort him a little."

"Good idea," Jim said. "I'm sure he needs sympathy."

Jim returned to the tool shed, and Clark started toward the corral. As the man approached the fence, Fury jerked his head up. Joey was startled.

"Oh," he said. "I didn't hear you coming."

"I always know where to look for you, son," Clark said heartily. "You're usually right here with this splendid horse of yours."

He climbed the fence and threw his leg over the top rail. At once Fury made a deep, menacing sound and flattened his ears.

"What's the matter, Fury?" Joey asked in surprise.

Fury danced nervously, then turned to face the man on the fence.

Clark grinned. "I guess I scared him, coming up so quietly." He extended his hand. "Fury, come over here —let me pet you."

Fury lowered his head and repeated the menacing sound.

"Hey, Fury," Joey said, "cut that out. This man's okay—he's my father."

Fury's ears still lay flat against his head. Joey pulled them up, playfully. "Come on now, be nice," he said.

Fury's momentary anger subsided, and he nuzzled Joey lovingly.

Clark shook his head in admiration. "That horse certainly is fond of you, son. He obeys you without question."

"He sure does," Joey said, placing his cheek against Fury's muzzle.

Clark looked down at the boy, sympathetically. "I suppose you'll really miss him when you go away with me, won't you, Joey?"

Joey bit his lip and spoke in a low, intense voice. "Yes, sir, it'll be just awful." He glanced toward the house. "I'll miss everything."

Clark nodded. "By 'everything' you mean Fury, the ranch, Pete—but especially Jim, don't you?"

"Yes, sir," Joey whispered.

"I suppose I knew that from the beginning," Clark said solemnly. He sighed. "Sometimes I wonder if I'm doing the right thing, taking you away from all this. I certainly can't offer you anything to match this ranch life."

"No, sir, I guess you can't. But, like Jim told me, since you're my real father—" he faltered, and his voice trailed off "—it wouldn't be right if we didn't live together."

Clark reached down and touched Joey's shoulder. "That gives me a great deal to live up to, son. But please believe me—I'll do all I can to make you happy." He climbed down off the fence. "Well, Joey," he said, "while you're working with Fury, I think I'll take a little walk. I'd like to do some thinking."

"Okay, sir," Joey said.

Clark turned and trudged toward the house. Before he reached it, he turned right and continued on until he came to an old wagon road which ran through a stand of scrub pines. While following the road, he took the letter from his pocket, glanced at it and smiled. A half hour later he reached the tall trees at the eastern border of the Broken Wheel Ranch. It was approximately the spot where Joey had seen him talking with the stranger the day before. Presently he stopped to get his bearings and gave a shrill whistle. Hearing an answering whistle from deep among the trees, he hastened in the direction of the sound.

As Clark emerged into a small clearing, the stranger was slouched on the ground, waiting for him. His saddled horse was tied to a tree. The man was heavy and rough-looking, and dressed in dirty blue jeans and a black shirt. His crude, insensitive face was covered with a three-day growth of black whiskers.

"Yer a whole hour late!" the big man announced gruffly, as Clark walked up to him. "Where the heck you been?"

"Working, Mac," Clark answered calmly. "Where've *you* been?"

Mac grew belligerent. "Whatta ya mean, where've I been? You know where I been! I been holed up in that crummy camp over in the ravine, that's where I been!"

Clark chuckled and sat down on a flat stone. "You sound pretty unhappy for a man who's had nothing to do for three days but lie around in a nice, comfortable camp. What's eating you, Mac?"

"Mosquitoes, that's what's eatin' me!" Mac growled, with an injured air. He extended his hairy arms and displayed large, red welts. "An' I'm tellin' ya them mosquitoes've been eatin' a whole lot better'n me." He slapped his stomach. "All I've et fer three days is that junk outa them tin cans."

Clark grinned. "I'm sorry to hear that. I've been eating some delicious meals. There's an old fellow named Pete over there at the ranch who's an excellent chef."

Mac grunted. "Aa, c'mon—cut needlin' me and git down to business. How come yer so late gittin' here?"

"I was waiting for a chance to walk back here without being seen." Clark grew serious. "We're too close to the payoff to foul this caper up by making mistakes."

The big man's eyes gleamed. "We're close, huh? Ya mean yer in real solid as that kid's old man?"

"Solid as this rock, Mac. It's going to be a push-over."

"Yeah? Then how come it's already took ya three whole days?"

"Listen," Clark said sharply, "I know my business. You can't rush a game like this. You've got to con the mark until he's ripe. Then he'll fall of his own accord."

Mac shook his head, doubtfully. "But what if he don't? If Newton ever checks up on them Clark papers I swiped—an' that phony court order ya signed the judge's name to—"

Clark held up his hand. "Stop worrying. That court order of mine would even fool the judge whose name I forged on it."

Mac laughed. "Yeah—when it comes ta copyin'

names I gotta hand it to ya. Yer the greatest." He frowned and leaned forward. "But look—when *do* we git some action?"

"Today," Clark answered. "Look what came in the morning mail." He took the letter from his pocket and held it up.

"What's that? The phony real estate letter ya wrote?"

"Yep. Eddie mailed it from Kansas City, just as I told him to." Clark patted the envelope. "This letter's a work of art, Mac. If it doesn't touch Newton's heart, nothing will."

"Yeah, but when do ya spring it?" Mac was squirming with impatience.

"Relax, my friend," Clark said. "I'm going to spring it today, right after lunch."

Mac scowled. "What if Newton don't go fer it?"

"He'll go for it. He'll do anything to keep that kid."

"Yeah, yeah, but what if he don't? Have ya got that figgered out?"

Clark's face grew grim. "What's the matter, Mac? You losing your nerve?"

"No!" Mac boomed. "All I'm askin' ya is what happens if ya foul the deal!"

"Then we just pack up and pull out, and nothing will have been wasted but a few days of our time." Clark looked at his watch and stood up. "I'd better be getting back. You ride over to the camp in the ravine and wait there until the time we agreed on. And don't let anybody see you."

"Don't worry about me," Mac grunted. "I know my way around." He untied his horse and prepared to mount.

"Before you go," Clark said, "have you got the plans all straight?"

"Sure,"

"Well, let me go over them once again, just to be certain. If this deal doesn't pan out I don't want to be the goat." Clark spoke slowly, as though he were explaining to a child. "If the deal works, I'll go into town on the valley bus. But wait for me at the camp till five o'clock. If I'm not there by that time you'll know that everything has panned out, and you can pack up and meet me tonight at the hotel in town." Clark paused. "Understand so far?"

"Sure. An' if it don't pan out?"

Clark shrugged. "In that case I'll have to 'borrow' one of Newton's horses and high-tail it for the camp. You be waiting there, saddled and ready to move, because we'll have to get away fast." He put his hand out. "Wish me luck."

Mac took the hand and grinned. "Do it good, pal. I can sure use the loot."

"Don't worry, you'll get it."

Mac mounted his horse and rode away through the trees. Clark watched him for a moment, then turned and walked back toward the ranch.

CHAPTER 14

Clark Talks Business

AT THE LUNCHEON TABLE, no one but Clark seemed to have any appetite. An atmosphere of deep melancholy had descended upon the room. For Joey's last meal at the ranch, Pete had broiled thick, juicy T-bone steaks over charcoal. Joey drew his knife listlessly through the charred crust into the tender, pink meat and ate only a few mouthfuls. Jim and Pete managed to swallow only a very little more. Clark, however, ate every last morsel of his steak, then gnawed hungrily on the bone. Finally, as the other three watched him in almost complete silence, he devoured a wide wedge of apple pie and gulped two cups of coffee.

When Clark appeared at last to have had his fill, Jim suggested gravely that they all go out to the porch and sit for a little while. They filed silently through the door and took seats. Pete sat opposite Clark, glaring at him reproachfully, but Clark carefully avoided the old fellow's hostile eyes. Joey had taken a seat on the top step, with his back turned toward the men. Aware of the boy's pathetic despondency, Jim reached down and laid a hand on his shoulder.

"Come on, Joey," he said hoarsely, "try to cheer up. It isn't as though you were never going to see us again. The year will pass before you know it, and, if your dad will let you, you can come out next summer and spend your whole vacation with us."

"I certainly will let him," Clark said pleasantly. "That's a great idea, isn't it, son?"

"Yes, sir," Joey murmured. He turned to Jim, dolefully. "But, Jim—a year's an awful long time, and —maybe Fury'll forget me by then."

"Fury could never forget *you*," Jim said, forcing a smile. "Horses have surprisingly good memories."

Joey stood up. "Is it okay if I go now?" His eyes were brimming. "I promised Peewee I'd ride over to his ranch and say good-by."

"Certainly," Jim said. "Run along."

As Joey bounded from the porch steps, Clark called after him. "Try to be back by three, son. We don't want to get too late a start."

Joey nodded without answering. As the men watched him racing toward the corral, Pete blew his nose vigorously and moved toward the door.

"Reckon I'll go inside an' manicure them goldern dishes," he said.

After Pete had gone, Jim noticed that Clark had suddenly become pensive and solemn.

"Up till now," Jim observed, "you've been rather cheerful about all this. But now you seem depressed. Something bothering you?"

Clark heaved a sigh and nodded. "As a matter of fact, Jim, there is. I disguised my feelings as long as Joey was here, but now that he's gone I can speak freely." He took the envelope from his pocket. "It's about this letter I received this morning."

"Bad news?"

"Real bad news." Clark slipped the letter from the envelope and handed it to Jim. "It's from the real estate people who are handling that little house I told you about. They demand a down payment by

Monday, or I lose the deposit I've already put up on it."

As Jim scanned the letter, Clark watched him shrewdly. Jim shook his head.

"They say here they want a thousand dollars. When were you expecting to make the payment?"

Clark shrugged. "Well—I was hoping for a thirty-day extension. But now," he continued resignedly, "it looks as though I'll lose the house." He paused. "That means Joey and I will have to live in a rented room."

Jim scowled. "A rented room? That's no kind of a home for a boy like Joey."

"Of course it isn't. But what else can I do?" Clark assumed a shamefaced expression. "In my anxiety to get my son back, I'm afraid I exaggerated my financial status a bit." He dropped his eyes. "The truth is, Jim —I have no savings to speak of."

"In that case, I think you should have been more honest with me," Jim said bluntly.

"I know that." Clark looked yearningly toward Joey, who was just riding out through the ranch gate. "But, don't you see—I wanted my son desperately. It makes me heartsick to realize that only a thousand dollars stands in the way of giving my boy a decent home." He crushed the letter into his pocket and looked at Jim, pleadingly. "Jim, I feel sure that you love Joey almost as much as I do." He paused. "So— for his sake—can you help me out—temporarily?"

Jim looked steadily into Clark's eyes, considering his surprising appeal for assistance. After a few seconds, it seemed to Jim that the man's eyes wavered slightly, and Jim detected a certain hardness in them that was inconsistent with his "loving father" attitude. A shocking premonition suddenly leaped into Jim's mind.

"Come inside," he said finally. "Maybe we can work something out."

As Clark followed Jim into the house, a sly smile twisted the corners of his mouth. They took seats on opposite sides of Jim's desk, and Jim spoke in a businesslike manner.

"Clark, even if I were to lend you the thousand for the down payment, there's no assurance that you can make future payments. You've admitted that you have no savings. Won't you be heavily overloaded?"

Clark nodded soberly. "Yes, there is that possibility, and it worries me considerably." He sighed. "In my desire to have my son back, I suppose I was overoptimistic."

"It seems to me," Jim continued, "that Judge Morris should have examined your financial status more thoroughly before signing the court order."

At the mention of the judge's name, Clark's eyes flickered warily.

"Well—uh—" he began, groping for a suitable reply, "I told the judge that I had a steady income from the leather company, and he seemed satisfied."

"He must have been satisfied," Jim said. "Well—I know next to nothing about legal matters, so that's that." He toyed with a pencil for a moment. "Clark," he said presently, "I'd do a great deal to insure Joey's future happiness. But I'd be doing neither one of you a favor if I helped you get in over your head." He dropped the pencil. "I'm sorry, but I think it would be unwise to lend you the money."

Clark appeared crestfallen. "I'm sorry, too. It means that I'll be taking Joey into rather dismal surroundings."

"You're not obliged to take him away, you know." Jim leaned forward. "Look," he suggested, "why not let Joey stay on the ranch until you're better prepared to take care of him?"

Clark held up his hand. "Oh, no, Jim—that's very generous of you, but my heart's set on having him with me. Now that I've learned to know him and love him, I don't see how I could ever part with him again."

"Do you think that's being entirely fair to Joey?"

"Perhaps not." Clark assumed a martyr's tone. "Maybe I ought to give him up permanently—disappear again—go out of his life forever."

Jim eyed the man, keenly. "I hadn't thought of that possibility—but now that you mention it, it might not be such a bad idea."

Clark looked melancholy. "I agree with you, Jim, although it would mean the end of all my dreams." He cleared his throat and looked at the ceiling. "Have you any concrete suggestions that might make such a sacrifice—how shall I put it—less painful?"

Jim smiled, grimly. "I was wondering when you were going to get around to that."

"What do you mean?" Clark asked, innocently.

"That last speech of yours was just a little too melodramatic. And corny, too, I might add." Jim slapped the desk. "The truth is," he said caustically, "you came here fully prepared to give up your paternal rights for a price! All this real estate bunk was just a buildup to arouse my sympathy!"

Clark dropped his melancholy mask and smiled. "You're a very smart man. I think we understand each other."

"Yes, I believe we do." Jim opened a drawer and drew out his checkbook. "What figure have you got in mind?"

Clark shrugged. "Well, I'm not a greedy man, so shall we say—uh—ten thousand dollars?"

"Why not?" Jim answered sarcastically. "That isn't such a high price—for the outright sale of a son."

"I wouldn't put it just that way," Clark demurred.

"I know *you* wouldn't—but maybe Judge Morris would." Jim glanced at the telephone. "Of course, I could phone him right now and ask his opinion."

Clark was startled. "Now wait a minute! There's no need to call the law in on this matter—we can easily settle it between us. I'm sure we can arrive at a mutually agreeable figure, if ten thousand is too steep."

"It certainly is too steep. I don't have that kind of money lying around."

"Well, I'm perfectly willing to make a concession for my son's happiness," Clark said agreeably. "What amount do you suggest?"

"Before I can even begin to answer that I'll have to do some careful figuring." Jim took out a pad and a pencil. "Why don't you give me a half hour or so to work it out?"

"All right," Clark said, rising. "I'll wander around outside. I won't go too far away, so call me when you're ready." He turned and left the room.

Jim stepped to the open window and furtively watched Clark as he strolled toward the main corral. When the man reached the fence, he stood studying a group of range horses inside the inclosure. His right hand rested idly on a saddle which lay across the top rail. When Jim was satisfied that Clark was engrossed by the horses, he left the window and hurried to the telephone. When the operator answered, Jim spoke in a low, urgent tone.

"Now, listen carefully—this is an emergency. Get me Judge David Morris, in town. . . . No, he probably won't be at the courthouse, because this is Saturday. . . . However, you might try to reach him there first. He's just back from a trip and might be doing some extra work. . . . Yes, I'll hold on, but please hurry."

At the corral, Clark lighted a cigarette and took a deep, contented puff. He felt confident that before long he'd be riding to town in the bus, with a nice fat check in his pocket. Smiling in anticipation, he finished his cigarette and glanced back at the house. Suddenly, a thought leaped into his mind, and his smile turned into a frown. Whirling quickly, he ran up the driveway, treading the ground as lightly as possible. When he reached the porch steps, he bent down and tiptoed stealthily along the wall of the house, until he stood directly beneath Jim's open window. Jim's voice was distant, but his words were clear enough.

"Yes, Judge," Jim was saying, "he fooled me completely. I'm familiar with your signature, and it certainly looked genuine."

The man under the window broke into a cold sweat. He listened attentively.

"What about those other papers?" Jim was inquiring. "The birth and marriage certificates. How do you suppose he got hold of them? Could they have been stolen? . . . Well, Judge, it's pure luck that I found you there this afternoon. Do you suppose you could go to the files and see if there has been a theft? . . . That's very kind of you. . . . No, this is too important —I'll hold the line. . . . Right, sir, I won't leave the phone."

Clark had heard enough to realize that he had lost his money; now he feared for his freedom. He crept away from the window and dashed to the corral. Working in furious haste, he snatched the saddle from the fence and threw it over one of the range horses.

At that moment, Pete came into the dining room to put some dishes away. As he passed by the window, he saw Clark tightening the saddle girth. In the adjoining room, Jim heard Pete rattling the dishes and summoned him in a low, urgent voice.

"What's up?" Pete wanted to know, as he came through the doorway.

"Pete!" Jim whispered excitedly. "I've been the world's champion fool! Clark's a complete phony!"

"What?" Pete exclaimed.

"Sh—not so loud! It's true, Pete. He just tried to shake me down for ten thousand dollars! I called Judge Morris! He says he wouldn't have signed a court order without first consulting me. Clark forged the signature!"

Pete's eyes popped. "Why, that dirty, lowdown horsethief!"

Jim's words rushed out in a torrent. "He says Clark can't possibly be Joey's father or he would have acted legally. He's just a confidence man—a crook! The judge thinks somebody must've stolen those identification papers! He's checking the files right now while I'm holding on!"

Aroused to the urgency of the situation, Pete ran to the window. "No wonder he's saddlin' up!" he exclaimed. "Look, Jim—he's makin' a getaway!"

Jim dropped the phone, moved to the window and looked out. Clark was just riding from the corral, whipping his horse furiously.

"He must've heard me on the phone!" Jim cried. "Come on! He's not going to get away with this!"

"Not on yer life he ain't!"

Pete started for the door. Jim snatched his gun belt from a wall peg and hurried after him. As they ran toward the stable to get their saddles, Clark had already disappeared through the gate.

CHAPTER 15

Mr. X

JIM's roan was saddled and mounted quickly, but the calico pony was in a skittish mood and delayed Pete's departure for a minute or two. By the time Pete had emerged from the stable, Jim had already ridden as far as the gate, where he sat scanning the range for a sight of the fugitive Clark.

"See him anywheres?" Pete asked, as he pulled up beside Jim.

Jim shaded his eyes. "Nope—he couldn't have headed either west or north."

They looked to the south. A wispy cloud of brown dust was just settling among the scrub pines. Jim whacked his horse.

"Come on! He took the old wagon road!"

They swung around and galloped southward.

"He's got a good headstart," Jim shouted. "If he turns off into the tall trees it'll be a pretty cold trail."

"Yeah," Pete agreed, "but we'll be able to see where he turns off. That horse he's ridin' has got a brand-new shoe on his right forefoot."

"Are you sure?"

"Yup. I put that shoe on him myself, last Tuesday."

After they turned into the wagon road, they stopped momentarily to study the ground. Pete pointed to the sharp outline of a new horseshoe in the dust.

"That's it, Jim! That's the one to look fer!"

They started along the road at a gallop, riding side by side. Presently, Pete glanced sideways at Jim and noticed his gun belt.

"I noticed ya brung yer hardware," he shouted. "Ya figger on usin' it—that is, if we ketch him?"

"If I have to," Jim answered, grimly. "For all we know, he may be carrying a weapon, too. So be careful," he warned. "Any man that's low enough to pull the trick he did wouldn't hesitate to kill to save his own hide."

Pete's eyes flashed. "Doggone it! I can hardly wait t'git my hands on that road agent!" He made a fist. "It'll be a real pleasure to hang one on his eye!"

The outline of the new horseshoe was still visible in the dust at long, regular intervals.

"He's riding at top speed," Jim remarked. "I wish he'd picked a slower horse."

"We'll ketch him," Pete said confidently. "Don't fergit—he's a stranger in these parts, but me an' you— we know this territory like the inside of our mouths."

"Sure," Jim replied. "But there's plenty of canyons and ravines up there in the hills. Hundreds of places for him to hide."

"He can't hide fer too long, Jim. Even a crook like him's got t' eat, so we'll smoke him out sooner'r later." Pete looked up from the road and was amazed to notice that Jim was smiling. "What in tarnation ya grinnin' fer?" he demanded.

"Because all of a sudden I feel good."

Pete frowned. "Ya feel good? What about?"

"Up till now," Jim called cheerfully, "I've been so mad, I haven't given myself a chance to think about what's happened. But the truth just came to me." He glanced across at Pete. "Pete, do you realize that Joey isn't going to have to leave us after all?"

Pete looked blank for a second or two, then beamed. "Say! Danged if you ain't right!" He slapped his horse with his hat. "Ya-*hoo!*" he bellowed at the top of his lungs. "Jist wait'll Joey hears *this!*"

Suddenly, Jim brought his horse to a full stop and pointed a few yards to the rear. "There's where he left the road!"

They wheeled their horses and entered the woods, with Jim in the lead. After they had ridden twenty or thirty yards among the trees, they reached the clearing in which Clark and Mac had held their conference that morning. There was manure on the ground, among the many hoofprints which Mac's tethered horse had made. Jim examined the terrain with an expert eye.

"That manure isn't too many hours old," he said. "Pete," he added thoughtfully, "I wonder if Clark has a partner, and met him here not long ago."

Pete rubbed his chin. "Dunno—could be." He rode slowly around the clearing. "Lookit there," he said presently. "One set of hoofprints comin' in from the east, an' a whole mess of 'em goin' out in the same direction."

Jim kneed his horse over and leaned down from the saddle. "Yes, and here's the print of the new shoe. Clark rode out this way—maybe to meet the other man—if the man who tethered his horse *is* his partner." He slapped his rein. "Let's move."

The two men lowered their heads to avoid the overhanging branches and rode from the clearing into the woods.

When Joey rode Fury out of the ranch to say goodby to Peewee Jenkins, he turned south along the edge of the meadow, then followed a well-worn trail which led in an easterly direction through flat bottom land. The Jenkins ranch was situated about five miles away, in rougher country than that occupied by the Broken Wheel. The trail rose gradually from the flatland and threaded its way through hills broken by ravines and small canyons. As it descended again, it led directly to the Jenkins property.

As Joey entered the gate, Peewee and his parents were seated on the front porch. Peewee bounded down the steps, took Fury's bridle, and led him proudly to the house.

"Look, Mom and Dad!" he cried. "Here's Fury! Isn't he something?"

Mr. and Mrs. Jenkins greeted Joey warmly, then walked down to share their son's admiration of Fury. Both agreed that they had never seen a finer horse and that Joey had done wonders with him. Joey thanked them and dismounted.

"Won't you come up on the porch, Joey?" Mrs. Jenkins suggested. "I've made some cookies and a nice pitcher of cold lemonade."

"Thanks," Joey replied cheerlessly, "but I can't stay. My dad said I had to be back by three, so's we can get started. I—I just rode over to say good-by."

"We're sure sorry to see you go," Mr. Jenkins said.

"We certainly are," Mrs. Jenkins added, dabbing at her eyes. "But on the other hand," she continued, not very convincingly, "it's—well—it's nice that you're going to live with your father."

"Yes, ma'am," Joey murmured. "I guess it is."

"Well, Joey," Mr. Jenkins said, "I guess you'd like to be alone with Peewee for a minute, so Mother and I will say good-by." He grasped Joey's hand. "Good luck, boy."

Mrs. Jenkins gave Joey a tremendous hug. "Good-by, Joey dear," she whispered. "We'll all miss you."

"I'll miss you, too," Joey replied miserably.

After his parents had gone into the house, Peewee kicked a pebble, viciously. "Doggone it, Joey—I sure wish you didn't have to go."

"Me, too," Joey said. "It's gonna be just awful." He looked up at Fury, sadly. "Peewee—will you promise me something?"

"Sure—anything."

"I know that Jim and Pete'll take wonderful care of Fury. But they're awful busy running the ranch and—well, without me, Fury might get lonesome." Joey looked pleadingly at Peewee. "So will you promise me that you'll come over to the ranch every once in a while and—just talk to him a little?"

"Sure, Joey, sure I will," Peewee said earnestly. "I promise."

"I'll be back next summer, I guess. But please write to me. I'll send you my address. Write to me and tell me how Fury is."

"Okay," Peewee assured him. "I'll write often."

The two boys said embarrassed good-bys, then Joey swung into the saddle and rode away. A few minutes later, he looked around and saw Peewee waving and waved back. A short distance further on, the trail curved around a rock formation, and Peewee was no longer visible.

As Joey reached the top of a rise, half a mile along the trail, his attention was attracted by a man in the distance, mounted on a galloping horse. Joey recognized him instantly as Clark and wondered what his father was doing in this rough country and why he was riding so hard. As Joey watched, Clark left the trail and headed toward a narrow ravine. Deciding to investigate, Joey brought Fury into a canter. Within a few seconds, Clark had disappeared into the ravine.

In the ravine camp, Mac had taken down his tent

and was preparing to load it onto his packhorse. As he lifted the bundle from the ground, his saddle horse gave a low whinny. Mac dropped the folded tent and peered warily toward the entrance to the ravine. As he listened, he heard the sound of galloping hoofs. Crouching behind a rock, he peeped out as the rider crashed through the underbrush into the camp. It was Clark, covered with sweat and dust. His horse was lathered and breathing heavily.

"Mac!" Clark shouted in a desperate tone. "Mac! Where are you?"

"Right here!" Mac boomed, rising from behind the rock.

Clark leaped to the ground and looked back anxiously.

"What happened?" Mac shouted angrily. "You mess it up?"

Clark shrugged. "The deal fell through."

The big man grabbed his arm, roughly. "An' you was so smart!" he sneered. "You—the big brain—ya had it all figgered out!"

Clark pulled his arm free. "There's no time to talk nonsense—we're in trouble!"

"Whatta ya mean—trouble?"

"Newton's after me! Newton and his foreman!"

"How do ya know?" Mac demanded.

"I saw them."

Mac scowled. "They see you?"

"No. I doubled back, and they rode right past me." Clark spoke urgently. "Come on, let's get out of here fast. They know this country. They're sure to pick up the trail."

Mac shook his head, contemptuously. "You know what? I oughta hit you right on toppa the noggin! Ten grand—right down the drain!"

"Don't talk that way!" Clark said defensively. "No-

body could've played it smoother. But this Newton—
he's not the sucker I thought he was. Come on, Mac!"
he said impatiently. "We've got to get out of here, but
fast!"

Mac snorted in disgust. "What about all our camp
stuff?"

"Leave it!" Clark cried. "We'll be lucky if we get
away ourselves!"

Suddenly, the three horses jerked their heads up.

"What'sa matter with them nags?" Mac asked.

Clark put his finger to his lips and looked anxiously toward the ravine entrance. Both men now heard
a horse approaching. As they waited, warily, Fury's
dark form emerged from among the trees.

"It's the kid!" Clark whispered. "Let me handle
him!"

"Hi!" Joey called, as he rode into the camp and dismounted.

Clark managed a false smile. "Joey! What're you
doing here?"

"I was coming down the trail from Peewee's ranch
and saw you head into this ravine." Joey looked at
Mac in surprise. "Say—this is the man I saw you talking
to yesterday."

"That's right," Clark said. He dropped his pleasant
manner and spoke sharply. "What's the idea of following me?"

Joey was bewildered by the man's caustic tone.
"Why—nothing. I just happened to see you and
thought maybe you'd like to ride back to the ranch with
me."

"I'm not going back!" Clark snapped. "So turn that
horse around and get out of here." He waved his arm
impatiently. "Go on, kid—get lost!"

Joey was dumfounded. It was the first time that this
man who he thought was his father had ever spoken

to him in such a bitter tone. He turned to Mac in complete amazement.

"What's the matter with my father?"

"Yer *father?*" Mac guffawed. "Come on, kid, wise up," he sneered. "This character ain't yer old man."

"He's not my—" Joey turned back to Clark, astounded. "What's he talking about?"

"You heard him," Clark said disdainfully. "I'm not your father."

Joey was aghast by the man's cold statement. "Then —you just made up all those things you said? You told all those lies? What for?"

Clark looked at his watch impatiently. "You wouldn't understand if I told you. It was a business deal with your friend Newton—but it didn't work out."

"It sure didn't," Mac said. "An' if you're smart, kid," he added threateningly, "you won't make no trouble."

Joey was staggered by the impact of two conflicting emotions: the shock delivered by the sudden announcement, and the hope planted by the slowly dawning truth.

"I won't make any trouble," he said, finally. "I'll just go on home."

He placed his foot in Fury's stirrup and prepared to mount. Mac rushed forward and yanked him back.

"You ain't goin' no place!" Mac growled. "Yer stayin' right here till we make a getaway!"

Clark was apprehensive. "No rough stuff, Mac. We're in enough trouble already. Let him go."

"Are you crazy?" Mac exploded angrily. "If we let him go, he'll bring Newton an' the law down on our necks! This kid's stayin' right here! Gimme a hunka rope!"

Twisting suddenly, Joey broke Mac's grip and ran toward Fury. Mac plunged forward and reached Fury's side, just as Joey grasped the saddle horn.

"Get away from that horse!" Mac shouted, grabbing Joey by the hair and pulling him back.

Joey cried out in pain. "Ow! Fury! *Fury!*"

With a low, menacing sound, Fury whirled upon Mac and reared, ominously.

"Look out, Mac!" Clark shouted. "He's a killer!"

Mac gave Joey a shove which sent him sprawling to the ground, then fearfully raised his arms to shield his head from Fury's raking hoofs.

"A killer, huh?" Mac screamed. "I'll show him who's a killer!"

He made a dash for his camping equipment and pawed feverishly at his bedroll.

Clark was alarmed. "No shooting, Mac!" he cried. "It'll bring Newton right to us!"

Realizing what it was that Mac was searching for, Joe was terrified. "Run, Fury, run!" he called from the ground. *"Run!* Bring *Jim!"*

Fury glanced down at Joey, then turned and darted toward the entrance to the ravine. Mac had found the pistol and was drawing it from its waterproof case. Joey sprang up and threw his body against Mac's legs, at the instant Mac aimed and fired. The screaming slug tore a white chip out of a tree, not two feet from Fury's disappearing rump. Mac kicked angrily at Joey and fired another shot. The slug whistled harmlessly through the trees, sending down a small shower of leaves. When the echo had died away, they heard Fury's hoofs drumming down the trail. Mac uttered an oath and grabbed Joey's arm.

"That does it!" Clark said grimly. "Let's get out of here quick!"

"Okay," Mac snarled. "But we're takin' the kid with us. So throw me that rope an' don't gimme no arguments. We'll tie him on the packhorse an' take him along. That way, if we run into Newton an' the old guy, they won't take no potshots at us."

A few minutes later, the three horses began their climb up the tortuous ravine. Mac led the way and Clark followed, leading Joey's horse on a long line. Joey's hands were bound together, and tied securely to the saddle horn.

Jim and Pete had come up off the flatland to hard ground, and were circling their mounts in opposite directions in an attempt to pick up the track of the new horseshoe. As they completed their circles and came together, Pete was exasperated.

"Looks like we lost the track, Jim. Ground's too dang hard."

"We've got to keep trying," Jim said. "Let's spiral out."

As they separated again, peering down at the ground, they heard a faint crack in the distance. Both men stopped their horses and listened. Almost at once the second crack was heard.

"Pistol shots!" Jim cried.

"Yeah," Pete called back. "Up in one-a them ravines."

The men dug their heels into their horses' flanks and took off at a gallop toward the hill trail. Jim reached it first and gave his horse its head. Riding furiously, they sped around sharply angled bends and along dangerous ledges. As they reached a high point, the ravines and canyons loomed ahead, cutting darkly into the hillside.

Suddenly, Jim saw a black shape emerge from one of the ravines. It was Fury! Jim gasped and pointed. Pete, too, had seen the horse hurtle from the cleft in the hillside. Both men were seized with fear at the sight of the empty saddle and the wildly flying stirrups.

During their feverish search for Clark, neither man had given much thought to Joey. As Fury turned into the trail, running in their direction, the men urged their mounts to even greater speed.

Fury met the onrushing men at the entrance to the first ravine. His eyes were wild as he dug his forefeet into the ground and came to an abrupt stop. White foam dripped from his mouth and ran down the dangling bridle. The men pulled up short.

"Fury!" Jim cried. "Where's Joey?"

The agitated horse reared and danced crazily on the narrow trail.

"Joey!" Pete shouted. "Joey! Where is he?"

Fury pranced backward a few steps, almost losing his footing on the ledge. A slab of shale broke loose and rattled down among the rocks.

"Fury, go back!" Jim commanded. "Back! Take us to Joey!"

Fury threw his head up and neighed.

"Turn!" Jim shouted. "Turn!"

Fury neighed once again, then whirled around and sped up the trail. The men followed at breakneck speed, both fearful of what they might soon find in the dark shadows of the ravine.

High on the rough, overgrown trail, Mac was leading his procession through a narrow passage between solid walls of rock. Clark rode ten yards behind him, with the lead rope of Joey's horse wrapped around his wrist.

Since they had ridden from the camp, Joey had been working constantly to loosen the rope which tied his hands to the saddle horn. Although the knot had loosened appreciably, the sharp rope had cut into Joey's flesh, and his wrists were raw and bleeding.

As the ravine widened slightly, Joey stopped strug-

gling with his bonds and half turned in his saddle. He
was certain that he heard a sound some distance
down the trail. In a moment, Clark, too, looked around
in a listening attitude.

"Hey, Mac!" he shouted. "Mac!"

"Whatta ya want?" Mac called back.

"Listen!"

Mac gave a disgusted grunt and halted his mount.
The sound was now clear and unmistakable: a
horse was coming at a gallop. Mac dropped his rein and
fumbled at the saddlebag in which his pistol lay. Before
he could undo the fastening, Fury thundered into view.

"Fury!" Joey cried in delight.

The horse Joey was riding screamed in terror and
sidled toward the rock wall, throwing him from the
saddle. The sudden jerk on the rope loosened the knot
which bound his wrists, and his hands fell free.

Fury brushed past Joey and lunged at Clark's horse,
which reared and catapulted Clark to the ground. Mac
now held his pistol in a firm grip, and as he swung
around to take aim, Fury whistled and rose to his
hind legs. His forelegs raked the rump of Mac's horse,
causing the animal to react so violently that Mac was
dumped backward. The weapon flew from his hand
as his body struck the rock wall. Mac rolled away from
Fury's hoofs, his hand groping for the pistol.

"Fury!" Joey screamed. "Don't let him get it!"

As Mac's fingers curled around the butt of his gun,
Jim and Pete galloped onto the scene. A wave of relief swept over them as they saw Joey, alive and
prancing with excitement.

"Look out!" Joey shouted. "He's got a gun!"

Jim vaulted from his saddle and landed squarely in
the middle of Mac's stomach. At the same moment,
Pete made a dive at Clark, who was just struggling to
his feet. Mac cried out in pain as Jim bent his arm back

and wrenched the pistol from his hand. Jim sat on Mac's stomach and looked toward Pete, who was joyously pounding Clark's face into the dirt.

"Atta boy, Pete!" Joey shouted happily. Certain that Pete had the man under control, he ran to Jim. "Jim!" he said breathlessly. "That man isn't my father at all! He told me so!"

"I know, Joey," Jim said, grinning. "Isn't it wonderful?" He glanced back at Pete, who was still punishing Clark's face. "Hey, Pete," he called. "That's enough. Leave something for the sheriff to recognize."

Pete rose from his victim and dusted his hands in high glee. "I don't know your real name, buster," he said to the moaning man. "I know it ain't Clark, but it don't make a bit of difference. When they stick you in jail, you ain't gonna be nothin' but a number!"

Jim jerked Mac to his feet and shoved him toward his horse. "Get aboard!" he commanded.

Mac climbed sullenly into the saddle. Jim turned to the con man and motioned with Mac's gun. "You, too, Mr. X."

The man who had called himself Clark mounted his horse, painfully.

Jim put an arm around Joey's shoulder. "Are you all right, son?" he asked.

Joey grinned broadly. "Sure, *Dad,*—I feel just wonderful."

Fury ambled up behind Joey and gave him a gentle nudge with his muzzle.

"Okay, Fury," Joey said tenderly. "You don't have to remind me. I'm sure ready to go back home."

CHAPTER 16

Bart's Showdown

IN RESPONSE to a telephone call from Jim Newton, the sheriff and his deputy drove out to the Broken Wheel Ranch and took the two culprits into custody. Upon being questioned, the prisoners admitted their guilt in the attempted shakedown. Both men were found to have prison records. Clark, whose actual name was Fred Kline, had been a forger and confidence man; Mac, whose full name was Jake McClurg, had served time for hijacking and armed robbery. In their earlier days, both Kline and McClurg had been floating ranch workers in various parts of the West and had gained unsavory reputations wherever they had been employed. At the county prison, they were booked on charges of attempted extortion and held pending trial.

The story of Joey's resurrected "father" had been widely circulated throughout the valley by the school-children, and Joey was impatient to spread the news that he would not be forced to leave the Broken Wheel after all. As soon as the sheriff and his man had driven away with their prisoners, he settled himself on the floor with Jim's telephone and made a dozen calls to his enthralled classmates. Peewee, of course, was the first one to receive the good news, and he and his parents were delighted. Peewee then took possession of his father's telephone to pass the story on to his friends. Naturally, every youngster who heard the news was eager to inform numerous others, and before long there was scarcely a telephone in the entire valley available to an adult. No one seemed to mind the inconvenience, however, for Joey was popular among his classmates, and Jim Newton was liked and respected by his fellow ranchers.

When Charlie Stevens heard the news, he immediately planned a celebration in town, with Joey as his guest of honor. Stevens had long wanted to do something pleasant for Joey, to atone in part for his stubborn actions in the white killer incident, which had almost led to Fury's destruction and Joey's complete despair. The celebration was planned for the following Saturday and was to consist of a visit to the county fair in the afternoon, followed by a dinner at the finest restaurant in town. As Jim and Pete had also been invited, Joey looked forward to the event the whole week long.

Saturday turned out to be crisp and clear—a perfect day for an autumn fair. After the morning chores had been completed, and everyone was dressed in his best, Joey walked down to Fury's corral to see that he was well and comfortable.

"Take it easy today, Fury," he said lovingly. "We'll all be back before it gets dark."

Fury whinnied softly and caressed Joey with his muzzle. Jim and Pete rolled slowly down to the corral in the station wagon.

"Ready, Joey?" Jim called.

"I sure am." Joey gave Fury a farewell pat, climbed over the fence, and seated himself beside Pete. "I hope Fury won't miss me too much," he said.

Pete chuckled. "If you ast me, that horse'll appreciate a day off."

"Yes, I guess he will. But I got Hank to promise

that he'd come down and say hello to him a couple of times while I'm gone."

Jim stepped on the pedal, and as the car drove through the gate Joey looked back.

"Where's Bart?" he asked anxiously.

"He went to town early this morning," Jim replied. "Don't you remember? This is his day off."

Joey looked relieved. "Oh, that's right, I forgot." He settled back and smiled. "Boy! A county fair! I've never been to one."

"Yer gonna have the time-a yer life," Pete grinned. "Yer Charlie's guest of honor."

"I know," Joey said, wide-eyed. "Boy!"

Jim turned into the dirt road that led to the main highway, and a short while later the station wagon joined the whizzing parade of cars which were headed for the county fair.

On his days off from the Broken Wheel, Bart always followed one unchanging program: he rose early, rode to town on his cow pony, and spent the day in Will Swain's Railroad Tavern and Pool Palace. If there was one activity that Bart liked better than eating, it was shooting pool. Having been a drifting bronc-buster all his life, he had lived through many periods of unemployment, and during those lean days he had managed to subsist by shooting pool for what he called "eatin' money." As a result of countless hours of practice at the green table, he had become every bit as skillful with a cue as with a lariat.

It was still early when Bart arrived at Will Swain's place, but the short-order cook was already on duty. Bart took his regular table by the front window and ordered a slab of fried ham, six poached eggs, a stack of buttered toast and a large pot of coffee. While eating, he kept a close watch on the other customers who came and went. Now and then, as acquaintances passed his table, he acknowledged their greetings with a grunt and a wave of his fork.

After he had finished breakfast, Bart propped his feet up on the brass curtain pole and settled back to pick his teeth. While thus engaged, Sammy, the rack boy, came in and went back into the poolroom to begin his duties. Sammy's work consisted of digging the balls from the pockets of the tables after each game and racking them up in the wooden triangle in preparation for the next game.

Six or seven men drifted back into the dimly lighted room, and soon the hum of voices and occasional bursts of laughter were punctuated by the sharp clicking of pool balls. Presently, a tall, gangling man entered the tavern and greeted Bart. Bart took his feet down off the brass pole and flicked his toothpick into a corner.

"Where ya been?" he growled.

The thin man shrugged. "A boxcar of feed came in this mornin'. The crummy foreman made me stay and help unload it."

The newcomer was Stew Crocker, a cowhand who was employed on the Pierce Ranch, five miles east of the town. His day off usually coincided with Bart's, and it was the habit of the two men to meet at Swain's and shoot pool all day long. Crocker and Bart were drawn together because of their almost equal skill at the game, and because each man recognized in the other a streak of cruelty and a hearty contempt for most of the human race.

Bart and Crocker moved into the back room and ordered Sammy to rack up the balls on their favorite table. They played rotation pool all morning for fifty cents a game, and when they finally stopped for lunch, Bart was nine dollars ahead. Crocker, who was a poor loser, wolfed his pork chops in grim silence. Bart, elated by his success, irritated his opponent still further by taunting him about being off his game.

Because of his anger, Crocker's skill deserted him completely during the afternoon. By dinnertime he owed Bart close to twenty dollars. Finally, Bart threw down his cue and laughed uproariously.

"That's enough," he boomed. "I quit. Playin' this game with you is like takin' candy from a baby."

The irate Crocker picked up the cue ball and flung it at the rack boy, who ducked just in time to avoid a serious injury. The man's vicious display of temper sent Bart into a paroxysm of laughter.

"Come on, Crocker," he gasped. "Pay up, an' let's git sumpin' to eat."

Crocker raised his pool cue menacingly, grasping it so tightly that his knuckles went white.

"Better put that stick down," Bart said mockingly. "You can't hit nothin' with it, anyways—not even a cue ball."

Crocker's face turned purple. "You fat bum!" he roared. "You been needlin' me all day!" He thrust his chin forward. "Like takin' candy from a baby, huh? Lissen, you big bum—how about playin' one more game—double'r nothin'?"

Bart shook his head and grinned. "Nup, it's too easy. I kin beat you any time—at anything."

Crocker slammed the cue onto the table. "That's mighty big talk," he sneered, "fer a guy that calls himself a buster an' can't even git close to that wild stallion out at Newton's ranch!"

Bart's eyes blazed. "What're ya talkin' about?" he said ominously.

"You know what I'm talkin' about—word gits around! That black horse out at the BW—that Fury! He made a bum outa you—but I hear that little kid

rides him alla time! You can't even lay a hand on
that horse—an' ya know why? 'Cause yer scared of
him!" Crocker nodded vigorously. "Yeah! When it
comes to gittin' anywheres near that horse, yer plumb
yella!"

Bart was breathing heavily. "Lissen, you skinny rat!"
he rasped. "There ain't a horse on four legs that I
can't bust an' ride!"

"Exceptin' one," Crocker sneered. "Fury! That stallion'd back ya against the fence an' tear ya apart!"

Bart glanced at the clock on the wall. "Okay, bigmouth," he muttered. "Newton an' them others is off
the ranch today, so there won't be no trouble. Git
yer horse an' ride out with me—right now! Ride out an'
watch me!" He took out his bankroll. "Ya owe me
about twenny bucks awready—an' I got another
twenny right here that says I'll fork that stallion an'
ride him!"

Crocker's eyes gleamed. "Now who's a bigmouth?"
He grinned, crookedly. "Okay, cowboy—you got
yerself a bet!"

When Bart and Crocker turned into the Broken
Wheel, the sun had already set behind the mountain range, but about a half hour of daylight remained. Leaving his companion to tether the horses
near Fury's corral, Bart walked up to the bunkhouse,
where he found Hank looking at a noisy murder show
on television. Hank raised a hand in greeting and returned to his watching. Bart took his rope from a peg
and went out. As he passed the woodpile, he picked
up a long, clublike piece of cedar and thrust it
under his arm. When Bart arrived at the corral, Crocker was standing a few feet from the fence, and Fury
was eying him suspiciously.

"This here's quite a hunk-a horse," Crocker said tauntingly. "Looks like a mankiller to me."

"I'll tame him," Bart said, as he began to unsaddle his horse. "I got ways of handlin' mustangs that Newton don't leave me use." He curled his lip, contemptuously. "But Newton ain't here right now, so I'm gonna show ya sumpin' that'll make yer hair stand up."

Crocker chuckled in anticipation. "This I gotta see, cowboy." He pushed his hat back. "Sure ya don't wanta gimme the dough now an' save yerself a couple-a busted legs?"

Bart mumbled a few uncomplimentary words under his breath, lifted the saddle from his horse, and hung it across the top rail. Fury watched warily, as Bart hurled his club into the corral, then climbed up and threw a leg over the fence.

"Where do ya want the body sent?" Crocker called, from a safe distance.

"Jest keep yer mouth shut an' watch this," Bart growled back.

As Bart was preparing his loop, Fury danced back and forth, with his ears bent flat against his head. Bart noticed the stallion's suddenly bared teeth and broke into a cold sweat.

"Okay, bigmouth," Crocker shouted. "I'm waitin' to see the great buster git busted."

"Aah, drop dead!" Bart muttered.

Taking a deep breath, he dropped into the corral. Fury jerked his head up and stomped the ground with his forefeet. Just as Bart raised his loop, Fury gave a sharp whistle and lunged forward, intent upon running the man down. In his nervous haste, Bart snarled his rope and panicked. Turning quickly, he scaled the fence with the speed of a monkey and dropped down on the outside.

Crocker howled with mirth and slapped his thigh. "Oh, man! I wisht I had a movie of you, squirrelin' over that fence!" Bart didn't reply to his tormentor, but his face was an angry red as he pulled his rope in and arranged another loop. Fury danced backward to the center of the corral, where he stood in a challenging attitude with his tail bannered. A low, continuous rumble emerged from his deep chest.

When the loop was ready, Bart again climbed the fence and jumped down. With another whistle of rage Fury shot forward to the attack. Bart stood waiting, with his loop cocked. A second before he would have been run down, he jumped aside and shot the loop at Fury's forefeet. As the rope picked up the slim legs, Bart fell back and jerked the loop tight. Having been tripped at top speed, Fury crashed to the ground and made a complete turnover. Bart grinned with satisfaction as he saw that the hated stallion was momentarily stunned. Holding the rope in one hand, he leaned down and picked up the cedar club. In a moment, Fury regained his senses, and, with his sides heaving, attempted to rise to his feet. As the horse's hind legs dug into the dirt, Bart yanked the rope sharply, and again Fury's body thudded to the ground. As he struggled to rise, he shook his head wildly, striking it against one of the fence poles.

"Go ahead!" Bart shouted in cruel glee. "Beat yer no-good brains out!"

Giggling like a madman and oblivious to everything but vengeance, the sadistic bronc-buster made his way up the taut rope. When the frantic horse made an attempt to rip him with his teeth, Bart raised the cedar club and brought it down upon Fury's head.

The thud of the club as it struck was the last thing Bart heard for several minutes. A moment before he had struck the blow, the station wagon had turned in at the gate. Its occupants had seen the action inside the corral, and, before they could do more than cry out in surprise, Jim had slammed on the brakes and dashed from the car. After vaulting the fence like a gymnast, Jim had given Bart a judo chop at the base of his skull, just as the club had struck Fury's head. As Bart dropped senseless to the ground, Jim picked him up and heaved him over the fence like a sack of potatoes. Crocker mounted his horse and made a frenzied beeline for the gate.

Sick with fear, Joey clambered over the fence and knelt beside Fury. The dazed horse was nipping feebly at the rope which bound his forelegs together. Pete, who had dropped into the corral by this time, tore the loop open and slipped it from Fury's legs. Jim, white-faced with rage, was examining Fury's head.

"Is he hurt?" Joey cried. *"Jim!* How *is* he?"

"He'll be all right, I think. Skin's cut a little, that's all." Jim lifted Fury's head, gently. "Stand up, boy. Come on—let's get up."

Fury rolled over with a grunt and rose unsteadily to his feet. His eyes were slightly glazed, but he shook his head vigorously. Joey reached up and threw his arms around Fury's neck.

"Oh, Fury!" he cried sorrowfully. "I shouldn't've left you at all!"

Fury whinnied, then lowered his head and peered through the rails at Bart, who was groaning and just beginning to stir. At the sight of his torturer, the angry horse curled his lips back and emitted an ominous rumble.

"I'll look after that Bart critter," Pete muttered, as he started for the fence.

"Leave him to me!" Jim commanded. "Joey, you stay here and try to quiet Fury down."

Jim and Pete climbed out of the corral together.

Jim leaned over the moaning Bart and slapped him sharply on the cheeks. The bronc-buster's eyelids fluttered, and, as his eyes reached a sharp focus, he recognized Jim and threw his arm up to ward off an expected blow. Jim grabbed him by the belt and jerked him to his feet.

"What'd ya slug me with?" Bart muttered, rubbing the back of his neck.

"Shut up!" Jim ordered. "One more word out of you, and I'll use that club you used on Fury!"

Pete grasped Bart by his shirt front and shook his fist under the man's nose. Jim motioned Pete to step back.

"Lemme hit him!" Pete begged. "Jest one good sock on the nose!"

"No!" Jim snapped. "I don't even want his blood on this ranch!" He spoke to Bart between clenched teeth. "I told you last spring that any man who uses rough tactics on my horses gets half an hour to pack up and high-tail it! But now that order's changed! You get exactly ten minutes!"

Jim lifted Bart's saddle from the fence and threw it at him. Bart staggered backward, as the heavy gear caught him in the solar plexus. Jim swung him around toward the bunkhouse and gave him a shove with his boot.

"Get going!"

Bart slouched up the driveway, muttering abusive language. Ten minutes later, still fuming with rage, he rode out through the gate.

After Bart had left, Jim brought his medical kit to the corral and treated Fury's wounds. As Jim had suspected, the abrasions were slight, but no amount of cajoling and soft words could quiet the horse down. Fury danced about nervously and peered out toward the range, making small, angry sounds in his throat.

"What's the matter, Fury?" Joey asked anxiously. "You'll be all right now. Nobody's gonna hurt you. Bart's gone for good."

"Now, Joey," Pete warned, "don't *you* git riled up. Fury'll calm down okay, once it gits dark an' everything's quiet."

"Pete's right," Jim said. "Fury's been through a rough experience, and what he needs more than anything is a night's rest." He picked up his medical kit. "Pete and I will go up to the house now. You can stay with Fury for a little while if you want to, Joey, but don't stay too long."

"Okay, Jim, I won't."

An hour later, Joey joined the men at the house. "Fury's still jumping around and making those funny noises," he reported. "You sure he's all right?"

"I think so," Jim answered, "but if he hasn't calmed down by morning, we'll ask the vet to look at him. He's coming out, anyway, to treat those two mares." He ruffled Joey's hair. "You'd better calm down yourself. You've had a rough day, too."

By ten o'clock the ranchhouse was dark. Everybody in it had had a rough day.

When Bart rode out of the Broken Wheel, he headed south for half a mile, then circled back to the old wagon road. After tethering his horse among the trees, he climbed to the top of a rise that overlooked the ranch and sat down to wait. Bart had never hated anybody as much as he hated Fury and Jim Newton, and as he waited for his moment to get even, he pounded the ground in vicious impatience.

When the ranchhouse went dark, he rose and paced the ground for still another half hour before mounting his horse. When he was in the saddle, he rode straight out to the soft meadow grass, then turned and approached the ranch gate in silence. At the gate, he dismounted and tethered his horse, then crept cautiously up the road to the gate of Fury's corral. In the dim light he could see the restless horse, prancing skittishly along the fence. For some reason, Fury didn't seem to notice the crouching man. The eyes in his erect head were peering out toward the meadow, and his wide nostrils dilated as he sniffed the night air.

Bart picked up a handful of sharp stones that lay among the gravel, then reached out and slid the bolt which fastened the gate. As the gate swung open, Bart climbed quickly to the top of the fence, prepared to leap to safety on either side.

Distracted by the squeaking hinges, Fury glanced down and saw the opening in the fence. For a moment he stood still, seemingly considering his next action.

"Go on, ya black buzzard—move!" Bart muttered. Fury stood motionless, and Bart drew his arm back and flung the stones directly at his head. As they struck his tender muzzle, Fury snorted in pain and charged toward the man on the fence. Terrified, Bart dropped down on the outside. Fury crashed into the fence, then backed away and made for the opening. As the running horse emerged from the corral, Bart again clambered over the fence to safety on the inside.

To Bart's surprise, Fury made no attempt to attack him again. Once on the road, he raced toward the ranch gate and galloped out in the direction of the open range.

Bart loped from the corral, glancing over his shoulder toward the dark house. Apparently no one had been aroused by the disturbance. Outside the ranch gate, he mounted his horse and rode northward. As he jogged along through the darkness, he caressed the stock of his rifle with his wet palm.

CHAPTER 17

Fight to the Death

JIM'S practiced eyes swept the hardpan of the corral. "It's Bart's work," he said flatly. "There's no doubt about it."

"How do you know?" Joey asked miserably.

Jim bent down and picked up several sharp stones. "These don't belong in the corral—they came from the driveway." He pointed to a number of similar stones which lay near his feet. "See there? Just about as many as a man could hold in one hand and throw."

Joey winced. "You mean Bart *threw* those stones at Fury?"

"I'd say so. He must've opened the gate and thrown them at Fury to drive him out."

Pete held up his hard, brown fist. "Goldern it, Jim! You oughtn't to of stopped me yesterday when I wanted to sock him in the nose!"

Jim shook his head. "A sock in the nose wouldn't have stopped him from sneaking back last night and pulling this infantile trick."

"But what did he do it for?" Joey wailed.

"For revenge, I imagine," Jim said. "Bart's a good wrangler, but he has a mean disposition. I think he drove Fury out because he thought it would be a way of getting even with me for firing him."

Pete spoke up. "It wasn't only you he was sore at,

Jim—it was Fury, too. Fury never cottoned to Bart, an' that got his goat."

"Fury has more sense than I have," Jim said regretfully. "He wouldn't have anything to do with Bart from the very beginning, but I put up with Bart's moods. I should've realized that he was nursing a childish grudge against Fury and fired him long ago."

"If I had *my* way," Pete said bitterly, "I'd shut that no-good buster up in this corral an' heave rocks at *him!*"

Joey turned suddenly and began to climb the fence.

"Where are you going?" Jim asked.

"Up to the stable and saddle Cactus." Joey's voice broke. "I've got to ride out and look for Fury."

"Yes, Joey, I guess you do," Jim said understandingly. "But I think you'll find him not too far away. Don't forget—he's a saddle horse now—he isn't wild any more."

"I know, Jim, but I've got to find him just the same."

"Oughtn't we ride out with him?" Pete asked.

"We can't, Pete." Jim checked the position of the sun. "The vet's due here in an hour or so to treat those two sick mares, and he might need our help."

"That's right, I fergot."

Jim walked over to Joey, who was perched on the top rail. "Tell you what, Joey. You ride out and start searching. I have a hunch the best place to look first is over Indian Mountain way. After Doc Weathers has treated the mares, Pete and I will ride to Indian Mountain and join you. How's that sound?"

"Okay."

Jim patted Joey's leg. "Cheer up, son—you'll find him."

Joey sniffed and wiped his eyes, then jumped off the fence and raced toward the stable.

Fury leaped over a fallen tree trunk and walked across the soft grass into the mountain stream. Lowering his dusty muzzle into a pool near the bank, he drank eagerly of the cool water. He had been running all night long, searching the range and canyons; backtracking and circling; crashing through underbrush and plowing across knee-deep marshland. Each time he had stopped to raise his head and test the air, the frosty October cross winds had brought the challenging scent from a different direction, causing him to wheel and follow a new course. It was morning now, but his sharp senses told him that his enemy was close by and that the battle which he instinctively craved was certain and imminent.

The white killer stallion had returned to the valley from some distant range, and Fury had responded eagerly to his far-off cry of contemptuous defiance. Even if Bart had not given him his easy freedom, Fury would have leaped the fence again as he had done before. The violent treatment administered by Bart had not been the cause of Fury's excitement the previous night; his nervousness had resulted from his awareness of the killer stallion's presence in the hills.

As Fury raised his dripping muzzle from the pool, a sharp gust of wind blew down the glen, ruffling his matted mane and bringing the strong stallion scent which he had followed throughout the night but had lost during the early morning. Quivering with expectancy, Fury leaped to the bank and shrieked his battle challenge. The piercing answer of acceptance came instantly, carried on the breeze from the upstream highlands. With a joyful whinny, Fury plunged into the shadowy forest and galloped up the steady rise. Presently the light grew brighter in the thinning woods, and, as Fury thundered into the full sunshine of the broad plateau, his snow-white adversary greeted him with a jubilant scream and charged forward to meet him.

In this battle of stallions there were no sparring overtures; no wily feints and considered measurements of the opponent's strategy or fighting strength. The combatants crashed into each other, standing on their hind legs, with their teeth bared and their forefeet striking with lightning rapidity. Their shrill whistling was fearsome and deafening, and their anguished screams when hides were raked echoed and re-echoed from the rocky walls of the cliffs, half a mile beyond the plateau. As jaws came together in frenzied attempts to close upon vulnerable necks, teeth clicked with the sharp sound of a slapstick. When the forelegs grew weary the horses whirled quickly, and the hind legs hammered into ribs and hocks. Both battlers knew instinctively that if they were to fall to the ground they would be stomped and sledged by merciless hoofs and slashed by knife-edged teeth. Both stallions knew also that the encounter would not end until one or the other lay dead.

The battle raged for many frantic minutes, and, finally, as their hind hoofs cracked together, the white killer turned swiftly and leaped at Fury's throat. With a quick shift of his feet, Fury jumped sideways. The flashing teeth of his enemy missed his throat by a hair's breadth, slid down his body, and sank into his left foreleg. Fury screamed in agony and reared so violently that the white horse was thrown off balance. As the white released his hold, Fury whirled and struck out with both hind legs. The steely hoofs met the white's jaw with a pistol crack, and his head was thrown back with such force that his neck snapped like a dry branch. His legs crumpled beneath him, and he fell to the ground and lay still.

Fury had won the battle, but the deep wound in his

left leg was the price of victory. Bellowing with pain, he turned and attempted to limp away, but the injured leg would not support his weight. With a pathetic whinny, Fury sank to the ground, not far from his lifeless enemy.

Joey had dismounted to examine Fury's hoofprints in the bank of the stream when he first heard the distant screams of the fighting stallions. Vaulting to the saddle, he urged Cactus into the forest. He had read tales about the ferocity of stallion battles, and fear clutched at his heart as he raced upward through the dusky woodland. Before he reached the scene of action the clamor ceased, but seconds later he caught the chilling sound of Fury's pain-racked bellow. Just as he reached the plateau, he heard Fury's harrowing whinny and saw him sink to the ground.

He leaped from the saddle in horror and knelt at Fury's side. Nickering a soft greeting, Fury struggled to rise, then fell back, unable to stand upon his injured leg. Joey saw the blood oozing from the jagged wound and cried out in dismay.

"Oh, Fury! Fury!" he moaned, unable in his fright to say more.

Fury raised his head and glanced toward his fallen enemy. The white stallion's hide was flecked with red. The staring eyes and the grotesque position of the head gave assurance that he was beyond help.

Working in hysterical haste, Joey ripped off his shirt and tore it into ragged strips. Then, with infinite tenderness, he carefully wrapped the makeshift bandage around Fury's lacerated leg.

"There," he whispered. "Maybe that'll help a little." He pressed his tear-stained cheek against the soft, quivering muzzle. "Do you think you can get up now? Do you think you can walk?"

The prostrate horse rolled over and attempted again to rise.

"Try!" Joey pleaded. "Come on, Fury—try!"

Fury struggled weakly to his feet, but as he shifted his weight to the tortured leg, he snorted with pain and collapsed again.

At that moment a shadow passed slowly across Fury's body. Joey looked upward and saw two great birds gliding lazily against the sky. Choked with revulsion, he knew that the vultures could be patient but that he himself had no time to lose. Remembering suddenly that the veterinarian was visiting at the ranch, he sprang to his feet.

"Fury, I've got to go now. But I'll be back as soon as I can, with Doc Weathers. He'll fix your leg so you can walk."

As Joey mounted Cactus, Fury lifted his head and whinnied, as though he understood.

"Lie still, Fury!" Joey called. "I'll hurry!"

With an upward glance at the wheeling birds, Joey shuddered, then turned Cactus into the forest.

Bart had spent the night in Charlie Stevens' bunkhouse with the two ranch hands, Clem and Sam. In the morning, he walked over to the owner's residence and asked Stevens for a job as a horse wrangler.

The rancher raised his bushy eyebrows. "How come you want me to take you on? Did Jim Newton let you go?"

"Nope," Bart lied blandly, "I jest up an' quit."

"Why?"

Bart flushed. "Aah—lotsa reasons. Me an' Newton didn't git along—that's about the size of it."

Stevens noticed the man's shifting eyes and knew that he was lying. He had disliked Bart ever since the raiding incident, when Bart had secretly telephoned him that Fury had broken out of his corral. Because he had accepted Bart's information at that time, Stevens had almost destroyed Fury. Since then he had been ashamed of his own headstrong actions and loathed Bart for his disloyalty to Jim Newton.

"Wait here," Stevens said. "I'll consult my worksheet and see if I need another hand right now."

He went to his office and put in a phone call to Jim, who told him the truth about Bart's dismissal. Stevens then returned to Bart, told him about the call to Jim, and angrily ordered him off the ranch.

Bart rode away sullenly, with an even deeper hatred of Jim Newton, the man who in his mind was the cause of all his woes and adversities. Conscious of the fact that he would need to find work before the winter set in, he decided to look for it on the opposite side of the ridge, where Jim Newton was not so well-known, and where they would probably not check the reason for his being unemployed.

Muttering imprecations against the injustice of people in general and Jim in particular, Bart started up the trail which cut across the north side of Indian Mountain. As he gained altitude, he noticed the pair of vultures wheeling slowly above the plateau. A short while later, another pair flew in from the east and joined the lazy circle. Being in no particular hurry, Bart turned off the trail and headed for the plateau, curious to learn the reason for the gathering of the loathsome birds.

As Bart emerged from the woods, the scavengers, which had just glided to earth to inspect their prey, screamed raucously and flapped into the air. Bart's horse reared in fright and almost threw him from the saddle. When he regained his seat, Bart saw the two horses lying on the ground and realized at once what had taken place: There had been a fight between a white and a black stallion, and the white one had been killed. He moved his horse to the black one, to see if it, too, was dead. Upon Bart's approach, the black horse raised its head with teeth bared and tried frantically, but unsuccessfully, to scramble to its feet.

Bart frowned in complete disbelief, then threw his head back and howled with laughter.

"Fury!" he roared in cruel delight. "Well, I'll be a son of a horsethief!"

Chortling with glee, he slid from his saddle and grinned down at the helpless horse. Fury threw his head forward and nipped viciously at Bart's boot. As Bart jerked his foot back, the teeth fastened on his jeans, ripping them to the knee.

"You black buzzard!" he shouted. "This time I'm gonna fix you good!" He looked at the sky and grinned. "Yeah! I'm gonna fix you good—fer them hungry guys waitin' up there!"

Giggling foolishly, Bart lumbered over to his horse and drew his rifle from the saddle holster. He broke the weapon open and shifted it to his armpit, then thrust his hands into his saddlebag. Finally, he drew out what he'd been looking for—a box of rifle shells.

Joey and his rescue party reached the bank of the stream and turned into the woods, riding single file. Jim rode directly behind Joey, followed by Pete, and finally by Doc Weathers. Doc had a special platform built on his saddle to hold his medical kit.

"It's not far now," Joey called back. "But it's real rugged and all uphill."

Now the party was climbing steadily, through the dense forest growth.

"Hurry!" Joey begged. "We're almost there!"

He peered ahead and presently, as the trees grew sparse, he saw something moving in the bright distance. Soon he identified the moving object as a man in a blue shirt—a man who held something in his hands which glistened in the sunlight. Suddenly, Joey gasped, and cried out in alarm.

"It's *Bart!* Jim—*look!*"

Jim roweled his horse and plunged past Joey. As Jim emerged from the trees, Bart raised his rifle to his shoulder and aimed it at Fury, who was writhing in an effort to regain his feet. When Jim was only a few yards from Bart, he leaped from the saddle with his arms outstretched, and the bodies crashed together with a tremendous thud. The rifle flew from Bart's hands and clattered to the ground, near the body of the white stallion. Shouting curses, Bart rolled over upon Jim's supine body and clutched him by the throat. Jim bridged his back and twisted rapidly to the right. Bringing his legs up in a springlike action, he hammered his knees into Bart's stomach. Bart gave a loud gasp and released Jim's neck. Jim sprang to his feet and pulled Bart up by the hair. As the man howled with pain, Jim smashed his right fist into the open mouth, and Bart fell as though he had been pole-axed.

Pete threw his hat into the air and jumped like a cat on a griddle. "Yow-*ee!*" he cried joyously. "That was jest plumb wonderful!"

"He'll sleep for quite a while," Jim said grimly.

"Yeah, but I shore hope he wakes up before too long," Pete cried. "I'm jest itchin' to send him by-by agin!"

Pete retrieved Bart's rifle and emptied it; then took the extra shells from Bart's saddlebag and threw them into the woods.

Jim walked back to Joey and Doc, who were kneeling beside Fury. Doc had just finished cutting the stiffened bandage from Fury's leg.

"How bad is it?" Jim asked.

"The wound's deep," Doc said, "but it'll heal. What I'm worried about is a possible fracture."

Joey groaned and turned away. Jim knelt down and put his arm around the frightened boy's shoulder.

"Take it easy, son," he whispered. "We don't know yet."

Doc Weathers lifted the lacerated foreleg and flexed it gently. Fury snorted with pain, but made no attempt to pull away. The vet explored the bones of the leg with knowing fingers. Finally, he looked up with a pleased expression.

"There may be a slight crack here, but there's certainly no fracture."

Tears of relief welled into Joey's eyes. "Can I please hold his head?" he asked.

Doc Weathers nodded. "I think he'd like you to."

Seating himself on the ground, Joey lifted Fury's head gently and squirmed his legs in under it. Fury sighed wearily and closed his eyes. While Doc Weathers cleaned the wound, the patient endured the pain without making a sound.

"I know it hurts something awful," Joey whispered into Fury's ear. "But you're gonna be well again soon, and then we'll have some wonderful times together."

Jim spoke gravely to Doc Weathers, in a low tone. "How're we going to get Fury down off this mountain, Doc?"

"It's going to be a slow journey, but we'll manage it all right if we take the trail down the north side. We'll cut some splints, to give the leg temporary support."

"Will he be able to put his weight on it?"

Doc Weathers grinned. "Stop worrying, Jim. I've been doctoring horses in these mountains for a good many years, and I've handled plenty of cases more serious than this one."

Jim nodded. "I know, Doc. I was just thinking of Joey. If anything ever happened to this horse of his—"

"It won't," Doc said, with professional assurance. "This horse is in much better shape than that sleeping beauty over there. You gave that bronc-buster a real jawbuster." He called out to Pete. "Say, Pete—while we're cutting splints, why don't you ride back to the Broken Wheel and drive the horse van to the foot of the north trail? When we get Fury down off this mountain, we'll ride him back home in style."

"Okay, Doc," Pete said. "But, hey, Jim—what're we gonna do with this Bart critter?"

"We're going to let him go."

Pete couldn't believe his ears. "Lettim *go?*"

"Sure—he hasn't committed any actual crime. Leave him to me, Pete. When he wakes up, I'll let him know what'll happen to him if he ever sets foot in this valley again. I'll have every rancher alerted to give him the bum's rush. Now you'd better ride down and get the van. We'll meet you at the foot of the trail."

Pete sighed and looked longingly at the recumbent Bart. "Okay, Jim, but twice now you've robbed me of my chance to sock him. Danged if I ain't gonna picket the ranch, with a sign readin': 'Jim Newton's Unfair to Pete fer Not Lettin' Him Sock Bart!'" Pete grinned and tousled Joey's hair. "Good luck, boy. I'll be waitin' down yonder with the van."

Pete mounted his horse and rode off into the trees. A half hour later, Doc and the others coaxed Fury to his feet, and the rescue party began its slow, painful trek down the mountain.

During the afternoon, Doc Weathers had hung a body sling in Fury's stall, so that the patient could relax without resting his full weight upon his injured leg. When night came, Joey set up a cot in the stable, as close to Fury as possible. After the lights had gone out in the ranchhouse, the boy lay awake for a long time, gazing up at the magnificent stallion, who had given him his love and trust and with whom he had shared so many adventures.

In the morning, when Jim and Pete entered the barn, they found the cot empty. The men exchanged smiles, then walked softly across the wooden floor and peered over the gate of the stall. On a bed of straw at Fury's feet, Joey was sleeping peacefully.